"What if the baby wakes up?"

Hawk heard himself asking as Kate broke the spell of their physical closeness, going lightly down the stairs. "Would you like to stay for a while? Just to make sure?" *What the hell are you doing, Adams?*

Kate seemed to be wondering exactly the same thing. There was a huge question in her huge eyes, and it wasn't entirely without suspicion.

As if she thought he might have lured her over here to steal a few kisses.

Sure, lady, I made the kid cry just to get you over here because I haven't been able to get your lips out of my head for a week. His eyes went to her lips. It was true. He hadn't.

There was a funny singing inside him.

Lordy, Hawk, he asked himself, *what the hell are you up to?*

D0836904

Dear Reader,

What's a single FABULOUS FATHER to do when he discovers he has another daughter—a child he never knew about? Why, marry the secretive mom, of course! And that's exactly what he proposes in Moyra Tarling's *Twice a Father*. Don't miss this wonderful story.

This month, two authors celebrate the publication of their twenty-fifth Silhouette books! *A Handy Man To Have Around* is Elizabeth August's twenty-fifth book—and part of her bestselling miniseries, SMYTHESHIRE, MASSACHUSETTS. In this delightful novel, a tall, dark and gorgeous hunk sure proves to be A Handy Man To Have Around when a small-town gal needs big-time help!

Daddy on the Run is Carla Cassidy's twenty-fifth book for Silhouette—and part of her intriguing miniseries THE BAKER BROOD. In this heartwarming tale, a married dad can finally come home—to his waiting wife and daughter.

In Toni Collins's *Willfully Wed*, a sexy private investigator learns who anonymously left a lovely lady a potful of money. But telling the truth could break both their hearts!

Denied his child for years, a single dad wants his son—*and* the woman caring for the boy—in *Substitute Mom* by Maris Soule.

And finally, there's only one thing a bachelor cop with a baby on his hands can do: call for maternal backup in Cara Colter's *Baby in Blue*.

Six wonderful love stories by six talented authors—that's what you'll find this and every month in Silhouette Romance!

Enjoy every one...

Melissa Senate
Senior Editor

Please address questions and book requests to:
Silhouette Reader Service
U.S.: 3010 Walden Ave., P.O. Box 1325, Buffalo, NY 14269
Canadian: P.O. Box 609, Fort Erie, Ont. L2A 5X3

BABY IN BLUE

Cara Colter

Silhouette
R O M A N C E™
Published by Silhouette Books
America's Publisher of Contemporary Romance

If you purchased this book without a cover you should be aware
that this book is stolen property. It was reported as "unsold and
destroyed" to the publisher, and neither the author nor the
publisher has received any payment for this "stripped book."

In loving memory of my mom, Ruth Caron
1938-1995

 SILHOUETTE BOOKS

ISBN 0-373-19161-8

BABY IN BLUE

Copyright © 1996 by Cara Colter

All rights reserved. Except for use in any review, the reproduction
or utilization of this work in whole or in part in any form by any
electronic, mechanical or other means, now known or hereafter
invented, including xerography, photocopying and recording, or in
any information storage or retrieval system, is forbidden without
the written permission of the editorial office, Silhouette Books,
300 East 42nd Street, New York, NY 10017 U.S.A.

All characters in this book have no existence outside the imagination of
the author and have no relation whatsoever to anyone bearing the same
name or names. They are not even distantly inspired by any individual
known or unknown to the author, and all incidents are pure invention.

This edition published by arrangement with Harlequin Books S.A.

® and TM are trademarks of Harlequin Books S.A., used under license.
Trademarks indicated with ® are registered in the United States Patent
and Trademark Office, the Canadian Trade Marks Office and in other
countries.

Printed in U.S.A.

Books by Cara Colter

Silhouette Romance

Dare to Dream #491
Baby in Blue #1161

CARA COLTER

shares ten acres in the wild Kootenay region of British Columbia with the man of her dreams, three children, two horses, a cat with no tail, and a golden retriever who answers best to "bad dog." She loves reading, writing and the woods in winter (no bears). She says life's delights include an automatic garage door opener and the skylight over the bed that allows her to see the stars at night.

She also says, "I have not lived a neat and tidy life, and used to envy those who did. Now I see my struggles as having given me a deep appreciation of life, and of love, that I hope I succeed in passing on through the stories that I tell."

Officer Hawk Adams's Laws of Baby Rearing:

1. Seventeen years on the police force does not a daddy make.
2. Real men don't change diapers. (This rule is subject to change....)
3. A hungry baby's wail will get you moving faster than any police siren.
4. Don't panic—your baby is not shedding. Chances are those flakes are from the dried cereal you forgot to wipe off the little darling's face.
5. Never underestimate the beauty of holding a child—or the love of a good woman....

Chapter One

"The Lilac Lady," Hawk Adams muttered under his breath. "I don't believe it."

At least the chief had given him the unmarked car, he thought, without a great deal of gratitude.

He wheeled the car out of the small parking lot adjacent to the old, single-story, redbrick police station with the ease of a man who had spent a good deal of time in cars.

He drove slowly down the main street of Sleepy Grove and had to smile, a bit wryly, and remind himself his reality was different now. They did things differently here. Informal. Friendly. Unorthodox.

"Unprofessional," he muttered out loud, giving his head a slight disapproving shake. "Lilac Lady." He didn't know much about lilacs, except it seemed to him a scent that old ladies wore in distressing abundance.

No doubt she would be an old lady, probably wearing a faded purple dress and a turban with a fake diamond in the middle.

Out of the corner of his eye Hawk saw a man sprawled in a straight-back chair underneath one of the colorful permanent awnings that dotted the tree-lined main street. He gave Hawk a casual salute.

Hawk squinted at him. Who was that? The police force here only had four cars. He realized the unmarked car didn't give him quite the anonymity he would have liked. The man had acknowledged him simply because he was the law.

The smile touched his lips again—cynical and faintly disbelieving. People here liked the law. They still smiled and waved at their police officers. Little kids came up to him and stared at him with such wide-eyed awe it threatened some of the ice that seventeen years with a big-city force had encased his heart in.

Which was why he had come here, he reminded himself. To see if there was a heart left.

It had started as something of a joke. His sister and her husband had moved from Miami to Sleepy Grove, and he'd come on a brief visit when his niece was born.

"What have you become, Hawk?" his sister had asked him one night as they sat in the shade of her front porch, sipping iced tea and listening to crickets.

He didn't have to ask what she meant. He'd felt the changes coming in him for some time. A growing hardness, an inability to connect with other people.

He was a long way away from the idealistic young man who had become involved in law enforcement the day he turned twenty. What had happened to helping people? What had happened to caring?

His last three years had been spent undercover. He'd felt as if he was in a war and his side was losing.

"I don't know," he'd said to his sister, and for once the remoteness had been gone from his voice, replaced with a deep weariness.

"There's an opening on the police force here," she'd said. "Why don't you apply? You know the fishing around here is great." She'd said that as if her words cinched the decision.

He'd been with her for three days, looking cynically at small-town America, thinking it looked too good to be true. Not believing and yet wanting, with all his heart, to believe.

He'd applied for the job.

And hadn't been sure if he was delighted or dismayed when he got it.

Six months later, he still wasn't sure.

He sighed, then braked for a woman pushing her two-seated baby stroller across the street.

She waved at him.

Sleepy Grove needed a different unmarked car. He put the vehicle back in gear, driving slowly. He was in the residential area now, his window unrolled, his elbow resting on the door.

This part of town was pretty as a picture. Tidy little houses stood side by side, carrying their fifty and sixty years with the dignity that careful tending gave them. Each had an immaculate patch of lawn and a picket or hedge fence. Spring was lending her lacy green charm to a portrait that was already delightful. Pussy willows were heavy in the trees, and he could hear the roar of lawn mowers going for the first time of the season. The air was full of that smell of dust and dead grass. How could a smell like that hold so much promise?

He saw an old man, suspenders on his pants, carefully stringing his rows over the freshly tilled soil of his garden patch. At the sound of the car the man turned and waved casually.

Hawk touched his forehead in return.

Not that there wasn't crime in Sleepy Grove. He was starting to learn some of the secrets behind these neat houses. The mayor's wife drank—and drove. The high school math teacher beat his son up, not that they could prove it…so far. The old lady who lived in that pink stucco house stole lipsticks and laxatives from Herb's drugstore.

The high school kids gathered at the Square and drank beer from the trunks of their cars on Friday nights. And Sleepy Grove probably held the state record for unrepentant speeders.

There was an area of houses on the east side that weren't like these ones. Where weeds and old cars accumulated in the front yards, and where domestic disputes broke out with depressing regularity.

No, not a perfect town. But still, in six months, not one bit of police work he had done had made his heart race with fear and excitement and his palms glaze with icy sweat.

He hadn't yet decided if he liked that or not.

Besides, this case he was working on now did not have a good feel to him.

Two girls were gone, within a week of each other, both the same age, both blond, both blue-eyed, both slender, though Samantha was tall and Sadie was short. It might even be significant that their names started with the same two letters. If there was a creep on the loose, you never knew which of the common threads might end up having importance.

Nobody had thought much of Sadie McGee disappearing. She came from one of those east-side houses and was a loud girl who wore too much makeup and too little skirt.

He'd had a run-in with her once at the Square on a Friday night.

She'd told him, in most unladylike language, what she thought of cops.

But he wasn't one of the small-town boys she was used to dealing with, slow and easygoing.

He'd just looked at her. He hadn't said a single word. He wasn't sure what was in his eyes. His sister, who had a tendency toward the dramatic, said they were hard and cold like a killer's eyes, but of course she'd never seen a killer in her entire life. Still there was something there that had backed down major-league drug dealers on more than one occasion. Sadie McGee was just a little-league girl. He wasn't a man to be messed with, and it showed.

She'd backed down fast, and he'd seen, for a moment, her youth and vulnerability.

She'd disappeared a week after her graduation from school. But she was of legal age, and when he'd seen the inside of the house she'd come from, he'd sympathized with her disappearance. Her family wasn't quite sure how she happened to be gone—it was as if they'd woken up one morning and been slightly startled to find her missing.

But a week later Samantha Height was also gone. She was also a member of the Sleepy Grove graduating class, but aside from their physical appearances being generally the same, there were few similarities between the girls. Sam, as her friends and family called her, was everything Sadie was not. A straight-*A* student, a cheerleader, a doctor's daughter.

No, he didn't like the way this case felt.

The chief, roly-poly Bill Nordstrom, said not to worry about it. Both girls would show up. There was certainly no evidence of wrongdoing. And both girls had taken some things with them, leading Bill to believe they were off on "some sort of adventure."

Hawk wasn't so sure. He thought maybe the people here in this little town had forgotten what the real world was like, had denied that reality could ever touch them.

But it could. It could and it would, the moment they got too complacent, let their guard down too much.

The chief just looked slightly amused when Hawk said things like that, as if too many years on a big-city force had done things to his head.

Which it had.

For as much as he wanted to know what had happened to those girls, he resented Bill's suggestion that he consult the Lilac Lady.

He wondered if she'd have a black cat and a crystal ball.

Hell! A psychic. At first he'd thought Bill was kidding him along, but the more he'd resisted the idea of seeing the woman, the more Bill had dug his fat little heels into the plush purple-grape-colored carpet in his office.

So here he was, against his will, going to consult a little old lady with a turban and a crystal ball about police work.

His former captain would die laughing.

Ha-ha, he thought, pulling the car to the side of the road and checking the address on the house.

Here it was. An ordinary enough looking little house, not half a mile from his sister's, on one of those ordinary Sleepy Grove streets. Surprisingly there was no sign advertising she would read cards or talk to the dearly departed. There were no stars and moon hanging garishly over her door.

He took a deep breath and unfolded himself from the car. He breathed in deeply of the sun-warmed air, heavy with spring smells, and turned his attention again to the house.

It was a tiny place, plain and boxlike, finished in that stucco with the sparkles in it that had been popular around the time of Custer's Last Stand.

Still, there was something faintly welcoming about the place. It stood in the shade of a mature maple, and crocuses peered out from the flower beds. Tulip spikes promised more color to come. A thick hedge of lilac trees, just about to bloom, ran the entire western boundary of the yard. An old-fashioned swing, full of plump, flowered pillows, stood motionless on a side porch, and bright yellow curtains framed the windows from the inside.

Alert as he was, he saw no black cat. There wasn't even a crystal hanging in that front window, capturing the magic of the sun.

He went up to the front door. The inside door was open, the screen door closed. He was willing to bet if he tried it, it wouldn't be locked.

Sleepy Grove residents were indifferent to the wisdom of locked doors.

He rang the bell, listening to it chime within, taking inventory of what he could see through the open door.

Hardwood floors and scatter rugs, a plump yellow sofa with a magazine open on it and a nice watercolor above it.

A sea scene, not unicorns or wizards.

He'd imagined something darker. A house full of old things, intricate curios that needed dusting. He'd imagined a place that smelled slightly of must and mystery.

And this place did smell. But it was a faint, fresh scent of lemons that hung sweetly in the air.

He was probably at the wrong address. He rang the doorbell again and listened to it chime emptily through the house.

With relief he turned away from the door. He'd done his best. He'd tried. There was no one here.

Still, that open front door told him someone was probably close, and the stickler in him couldn't face Bill and say he'd tried, unless he really had.

He walked around the side of the house and looked over the gate to the backyard.

Sure enough, she was there, kneeling in her garden, her features hidden by the brim of a big, straw sun hat. She was either offering prayers to the goddess or weeding. He suspected she was weeding.

She was not dressed in purple at all. A pair of white shorts, smudged with garden soil, rode up on legs that were astonishingly delectable.

He reminded himself that Lucille Ball had the nicest legs in Hollywood right into her seventies.

He took stock out of habit, gauging, probing for clues to who she was . . . alert for the first sign of danger. It would be a long time before that habit left him. It had saved his skin more than once.

His eyes skimmed the rest of her figure. She looked to be a wee bit of a thing, though it was hard to tell because she wore a man's shirt, striped and huge, rolled up at the sleeves. Green gardening gloves that looked like monster hands hung at the ends of small, delicate wrists.

He allowed himself to relax physically. Mentally he was still on red alert.

Chief Nordstrom was a nice man but a bit of a bumpkin. Naive. Twenty-five years on the force here hadn't even slightly dimmed the open, friendly light in his blue eyes.

But Hawk Adams was a different story, and he wasn't about to be led down the garden path by some small-town soothsayer.

"Excuse me, ma'am." He opened the gate, which squeaked outrageously, and went through it.

She looked up, and he was aware instantly of his error.

The face under the broad brim of that hat was that of a young woman, not an old crone who told fortunes.

Auburn curls scattered around an elfin face, the faintly upturned nose dotted with red freckles. Her mouth was generous, the lower lip surprisingly full.

She looked . . . wholesome, he thought, searching for the word. A perfect small-town woman in a perfect small town.

"I think I'm looking for your . . . grandmother," he said hesitantly, astonished to find himself uncertain.

He had long ago learned how not to show his uncertainty.

She pulled off her hat and ran a gardening glove through her messy curls, leaving a rotting leaf or two in its wake. A grin split her features and turned on a light in eyes he suddenly saw were an amazing blend of gold and brown and green.

Maybe, he thought cautiously, she was a witch after all.

Kate Shea tried not to show her awkwardness at the sudden appearance of the big uniformed man in her backyard.

She guessed him to be six feet, but the authority of the perfectly pressed, light blue shirt and the knife-creased, navy blue pants made him look bigger. The gun looked heavy and ominous in the dark holster that rested on his hip, and a silver shield winked under the bright spring sky.

His arm muscles, tanned and corded, showed to perfection beneath the short sleeves of his shirt. His chest was broad and his shoulders as wide as a lumberjack's. This great breadth tapered to slenderness at his waist and hips, and his legs looked long and lean beneath the dark trousers.

An arresting man, she thought, pleased with her pun. It would be easy to take a man like this too seriously, to be intimidated by him. Her eyes drifted up and stopped on his face. Her fledgling effort to break through the intimidation of his presence came to an abrupt end.

His hair was dark brown, like newly turned earth, very short at the sides, thicker at the top where it feathered back. His face was acutely handsome, the features even, his nose scarred at the bridge, his chin faintly clefted, his lips carved in a stern line that was utterly masculine.

His eyes were steely gray and shuttered under dark slanting brows. There were no laugh lines fanning out from their sides.

There were walls up in his eyes. High walls that had not been scaled for a long, long time.

But then, she had walls of her own. Walls that also had not been scaled for a long time. There was no reason to feel so oddly... threatened by a stranger standing in her yard regarding her with an interest that was cold and professional, nothing more.

He was the new police officer, of course. She'd been hearing about him on and off, little breathless phrases overheard at the supermarket or library. A new bachelor in a town this size always caused a stir.

And one who looked like this could cause a whirlpool, never mind a stir, sucking in hearts and souls— She stopped herself.

"My grandmother?" she asked. She got up, her effort and dignity lost to a sudden shooting pain in her back. She stretched and pressed at her lower back with a heartfelt groan. "On the lam from the retirement home in Palm Springs, is she?"

She was pleased with her tone. Light and friendly, a perfect disguise for the hard hammering of her heart.

How long had it been since she had been this close to a magnificent-looking man?

She forced herself to walk toward him. She stopped in his shadow, looked up into the cool gray of those eyes and took off her gardening glove. She stuck out her hand and wished almost instantly she could take it back.

His big hand brushed hers, engulfed it, released it, all with a certain cool indifference. And yet the impression that was left deep within her was not of indifference, but of strength.

What had she heard about him? she wondered, wishing she'd eavesdropped with a little more interest.

Sexy was the only word memory provided her with.

And then, reluctantly, another morsel surfaced. That he was from some big city. Miami? Certainly the warm, golden tone of his skin was not common to natives of Northern Idaho after a long, cold winter.

The big city was there, just behind the cool mask he was showing her. Harsh. Fast. Perhaps even violent.

Why would a man like this come to Sleepy Grove?

"Sorry, I guess it's not your grandmother. I'm looking for Kate Shea."

"That's me," she said with all the lightness she could muster. "I'll save us both time and confess. I did it. I put pepper right up his nose."

"Whose nose?" he asked with interest.

"That dog that does it on my front lawn. Mrs. Measly's. He ran out of here yelping like his legs were on fire."

"I'm not here about an assault on a dog."

She wished he'd smile. She'd like to see what his teeth looked like. She hoped they were yellow and crooked as Mrs. Measly's picket fence. But she doubted it.

"I was just going to have some lemonade. Do you want some?" The words were out, and then she felt foolish. What little worm of loneliness had wriggled out from her inner depths to make that offer?

She could tell by his face he did not want lemonade. In fact, his face was telling her a lot of things right now, and one of them was that he had decided, before he even met her, not to like her.

And that was back when he thought she was somebody's grandmother.

What kind of man took a dislike to grandmothers?

"Chief Nordstrom asked me to approach you about helping us with a case."

Now she understood. She watched him silently. How carefully he had worded that, making his arrival here Chief Nordstrom's responsibility, letting her know without saying a single word exactly what he thought of the kind of help she might be able to offer.

She was hot and thirsty and irritated now by the prejudices that flitted briefly behind that handsome mask.

"Come into the house," she said stiffly, her lack of warmth now matching his own. "*I'll* have some lemonade and you can tell me what *Chief Nordstrom* would like."

She led him through the back door, which opened directly into her small, bright kitchen.

"Have a seat," she said over her shoulder.

She went through the hall to the bathroom, rinsing the fine film of garden dirt off her face and trying to get a comb through her uncooperative curls. She hesitated and then, hating herself for doing it, took her lipstick out of the medicine chest and applied a touch of pink to lips dried by the sun. She thought of adding a little blush, as well, but even with the protection of her hat her cheeks were pink.

Was that from the sun—or him?

She went back into the kitchen.

He hadn't sat down. He was prowling, looking at things, those eyes that revealed nothing also missed nothing. He held himself with a certain alertness, almost wariness, like a big jungle cat that had been hunted too often.

He turned to her when she came back into the kitchen, scanning her features with that same wary, gauging look, before his expression flattened.

She helped herself to a lemonade, ice-cold and fresh-squeezed that morning. She didn't offer him a drink again.

She was aware that her kitchen, which had always seemed amply large and bright, seemed too small with him in it, as if his formidable size was blocking the light from the window.

"Now," she said, sinking into a chair and tucking one bare leg up under her, "what can I do for you, Officer—?"

"Adams," he said. "Hawk Adams." He stood for a moment longer, as if making absolutely sure he was safe, and then scraped out the chair across from her.

"What an unusual name," she remarked, studying him over the rim of her glass. It was an unusual name. But then he looked like an unusual man, and the name was fitting.

Very fitting. He reminded her of a hawk—full of that restless energy, circling, watching. She was willing to bet he was a very good policeman.

He didn't fill her in on the origins of his unusual name.

"How can I help you?" she asked shortly, seeing he wasn't about to be drawn into small talk. His eyes were branding her a charlatan. He'd probably expected to find a crystal ball on her kitchen table and a caldron boiling away on the stove.

"I'm not convinced that you can," he said coolly. "I don't believe in this kind of thing."

"Far be it from me to try and convince you," she said with infinite uncaring. He hadn't expected that, and she felt a small ripple of triumph. He was not a man who looked as though he was easily surprised.

"The chief thought it wouldn't hurt to ask you a few questions."

"But you don't agree with him?"

His eyes were carefully hooded. He wasn't going to come right out and say he didn't agree with his boss.

"Two girls are missing."

She felt a familiar dread in the pit of her stomach. She kept her face as carefully blank as his was.

"We don't have any clues. There's no suggestion of foul play in either case, but it's a little disturbing."

She nodded.

"Their names are Sadie McGee and Samantha Height. Did you know either of them?"

She shook her head.

"You're going to have to help me," he said suddenly, gruffly. "I don't know how this is supposed to work. Now do you close your eyes and start moaning or something?"

She felt the insult of this remark, made in a sarcastic tone that was more offensive than his remoteness.

"No, I don't close my eyes and start moaning," she said sharply. "I'll need you to bring me something that belongs to both girls. A piece of jewelry, a watch, a ring. Something like that. Then I'll tell you whatever I can. It may be nothing."

She could see the cynicism in his face. She was not sure why she took it so personally. Many people were skeptical. Only a few years ago she had been among them.

"I'm supposed to go and ask those girls' parents for something like that?" he asked, almost to himself. "What the hell do I tell them I want it for?"

"That's your problem," she said smoothly, though her heart was rattling away inside her chest alarmingly.

"What does the municipal office pay for this service?" he asked.

She stared at him. "On second thought, I don't want to deal with you." Fiendishly, she added. "The spirits don't like you."

"Yeah, right," he said.

To her annoyance he seemed to think she'd meant that. "Tell Bill to come himself, or to send someone else."

He was looking at her narrowly. "Someone a little more gullible?" he suggested silkily.

"Someone a little less abrasive," she suggested just as silkily.

He got up from his chair. "I'll see what I can arrange."

It was perfectly clear he was glad to be off the hook.

She had to get in one final dig. "And tell Bill I'll charge a hundred and fifty dollars."

He nodded curtly.

"An hour," she finished softly.

An eyebrow arched upward, but nothing showed on that face, a face she suspected had been schooled for a long time to show nothing of what he thought and felt. If he felt anything anymore.

He turned to the door, and his hand rested on the handle for a moment.

"You should lock your front door when you work in the back," he told her softly and then was gone.

For an inordinate length of time she stared at the place he had filled.

Chapter Two

He'd managed to do in three seconds what twenty-five years of police work hadn't done, Hawk noted uncomfortably.

The twinkle was gone from the chief's blue eyes. Bill Nordstrom was not a tall man, though he made up for his lack of height by keeping an impressive girth. His hair was white, and usually, with the addition of a beard, he would have made an ideal choice to play Santa Claus at the Policemen's Christmas Party. Usually.

"She's charging *what?*" Nothing remotely merry about that question.

"She said—"

"She's never charged us nothin' before!" the bulky man bellowed.

Hawk didn't let the surprise register on his face.

"Son, did you make her mad?"

Hawk wasn't used to being called anyone's son. He stiffened and then relaxed. The chief was determined to make him a member of the Sleepy Grove family—whether he liked it or not. To his dismay, sometimes he liked it all right.

"I might have got her back up a bit," he admitted.

"Well, you go get her back, back down. A hundred and fifty bucks an hour. Sheesh!"

"She doesn't want to deal with me anymore," he informed his boss, trying to conceal his relief. "She said the spirits don't like me." He managed to say that without any expression at all. He had a feeling mockery would not be acceptable just now.

"The spirits don't like you," the chief said with a shake of his white curls. "What's the matter with you, Hawk? Don't you ever laugh at anything?"

"I don't think she was pulling my leg," he said tersely.

"She *was* pulling your leg."

Hawk was silent.

"She was probably pulling your leg about the money, too. She's a good woman, Kate Shea."

Hawk caught the faintly wily look that was sent his way and eyed his boss with startled suspicion. Twice now Bill and Wilma Nordstrom had had him over for dinner. The first time the town librarian, who looked like a *Vogue* cover girl and was conveniently single, had been there, too. The second time it had been a vivacious veterinarian—also single.

The third time he'd refused the invitation. It was bad enough having to deal with his sister's well-meaning meddling.

The truth was he didn't know how to care about people anymore. His heart was in armor, and he didn't know how to break it out and wasn't sure he wanted to.

He'd seen what a bad relationship could do to a good cop. He'd seen what a cop's job could do to the best of relationships.

A long time ago he'd made a decision. He'd married his job. He'd given it everything he had.

And, he had to admit, it had taken everything he had, sucked him dry, left him a lean, mean fighting machine so out of touch with his feelings he wouldn't know one if it sat on him.

Which was all right with him. Uncomfortable, untidy things, feelings were.

So what was he doing here in Sleepy Grove? In some ways it would have been safer to have stayed where he was.

"Go see her. Apologize."

He thought of her house, that neat kitchen and the smell of lemons. There had been no sign of a man about the place, and there were always signs. There had been no toys or clothes that would indicate kids, either.

Unless he missed his guess the Lilac Lady was single. Why did he feel a ripple of interest? It was those eyes, he guessed. Spellbinding. Which said it all. He didn't believe in spells. She did.

"You want me to apologize for not believing hocus-pocus has any place in police work?" he enquired politely.

"Closed minds have no place in police work."

He clenched his jaw tight. "Yessir."

"Hawk, police work ain't the same here as where you come from. I haven't drawn my gun more than half a dozen times in twenty-five years. I've never fired it at anyone. The job here isn't about cracking heads and dodging bullets. You're more likely to crack a soda here than a drug ring or a car jacker's head. Police work here is about knowing your community. It's about caring about your neighbors."

There was gentle reproach in those words. Hawk wondered how many indignant citizens had complained he wasn't very friendly.

Friendly was a feeling.

He didn't feel friendly, though at least he didn't feel as wired, as hunted as he had felt six months ago. Maybe in time he would become the kind of cop who did fine in a small town. He could make small talk with the old guys playing chess in the town square, pat dogs, coach the little-league team.

He became aware of a funny ache piercing a crack in his armor. He didn't like that feeling at all.

So then again, maybe he wouldn't do so fine in Sleepy Grove.

He turned and left the chief's office.

He stood on her front steps. The door was open the same as before, the screen closed. Out of curiosity, he quietly tugged on that outer door. He let it go when it opened an inch.

She didn't listen worth a hill of beans.

Not that he found that surprising.

Inside he could hear her singing. She had a terrible voice, tuneless and raspy, but for some reason he liked the sound of it. There was exuberance there that made up for the lack of talent.

At least she was singing a popular hit and not chanting incantations.

He rang the doorbell.

She swung around the corner, wearing pink shorts and bare feet. A man's shirt was knotted over her midriff. Her hair looked faintly messy, and her figure looked fine. In one hand was a feather duster.

"Oh," she said, stopping in her tracks, "it's you."

He wasn't sure how he felt about successfully slaying her Sleepy Grove hospitality in one five-minute visit.

"I'm under official orders to apologize." The shirt she had on was open at the throat, revealing the top of a lacy camisole.

"Is that right?" she said coldly.

He sighed. "Could I come in?"

She shrugged, folding her arms, the feather duster resting just beneath her chin and making her look as if she was being coy behind an exotic fan. "If you have to."

So much for coy. He opened the door. It squeaked nearly as badly as her gate. He stepped into her little entryway and then into her living room.

The bright yellow couch was the focal point of a room that would look full of sunshine on the grimmest winter day. The walls were a mossy green, but everywhere accents of that daffodil yellow splashed cheer about.

He wondered how women did this. His apartment of nearly fourteen years had never looked like anything but a box with furniture in it, and the place he'd rented here didn't show promise of being any different.

Maybe he'd see if he could get a seascape like that one above her couch, two children running through golden sand with a yellow kite dancing on the wind behind them.

Maybe he'd stop leaving a trail of clothes from the front door to the shower.

"This is nice," he said uneasily. His eyes moved restlessly to a framed eight-by-ten photograph above the bookcase. It was her, her hair much longer, looking wild and rumpled as though she had just tumbled from bed. Her head was thrown back with laughter, a fat baby trying to insert its fingers in her nose.

She looked different now. More mature. Not quite as carefree or laughter-filled. Back then she might have painted her toenails pink. Now he noticed they were un-varnished.

He wondered, briefly, who the baby had belonged to. "Look, I'm sorry about the other day. I'm not used to us-ing—"

"Hocus-pocus?" she suggested tightly when he fal-tered.

"—alternate methods in police work. It would have been, uh—"

"Made fun of?" she suggested.

"Frowned upon," he hedged, "where I came from be-fore."

"There. You've officially apologized. Very heartfelt. Now you can leave."

Her arms were still folded. He didn't think she knew the feather duster was detracting from her firm stance.

"Actually, I brought the items you asked for. I was hop-ing you'd have a look at them."

"*You* were?" Her eyes were too wisely focused on his face.

"The chief was. I'm doing my best to keep an open mind."

"I'm sorry that's so difficult for you."

"Sometimes it is difficult for me," he admitted.

Though his tone didn't change when he said those words, Katie felt the sudden change in him, a very faint flicker of something vulnerable in a man who seemed too self-possessed.

She scanned his face, but no emotion showed in those steel gray eyes. He returned her gaze unflinchingly. Slowly she held out her hand.

He reached into the breast pocket of the uniform jacket he wore today and passed her a small brown envelope.

"Come into the kitchen," she suggested. She held the envelope gingerly, dreading what it might hold. "Leave your shoes on."

He followed her through to the kitchen, his step firm and strong behind her on the hardwood floor.

"Would you like tea? It's made." She set the envelope on her kitchen table. It was antique oak, scuffed and splattered with a strange shade of purple paint that the lace tablecloth she had on it didn't begin to hide. Someday she hoped to refinish it. When that stripping gaze of his fell on the table she wished she'd already done it.

Which was why, she reminded herself, there was no man in her life. Amazing how quickly you started doing things to make an impression on *him* rather than to make yourself happy.

He was still hesitating over the tea.

"It's made with a bag," she said, needling him, but he only looked puzzled.

"No leaves to read after," she said wryly.

A small smile twisted at the stern lines of his mouth. She caught the faintest glimpse of teeth that were straight and sparkled whiter than sunlit snow. It looked as though if he really smiled, a dimple would crease deep into his right cheek.

"Thank you. Some tea would be nice."

Her palms had started to sweat. Was it because of him? Or because of that envelope that sat on the kitchen table, waiting?

He sat down in the same place he had sat last time. Absently he stroked the petal of a white daisy in the vase in the middle of the table. For a moment she stared, mesmerized. His big hands were in sharp contrast to the delicate fronds of the spring bouquet she'd splurged on at the supermarket.

Unbidden, her mind wondered what hands like that, hands so strong, so sure, would feel like, their strength tempered, on a woman's—

Stunned with the wayward direction of her thoughts, she turned abruptly to her kitchen counter, putting milk and honey on a tray with as much concentration as a monk gives his meditation.

Finally she could avoid him and her awareness of him no longer. She brought the tray laden with tea things and fresh cookies over and set it on the table.

She sat down, poured and took a deep breath. "It's rose hip," she said, stalling. "No bat's wings today."

She could tell by the look on his face rose hips and bat wings were about the same thing to him. He'd drink coffee, black and thick as syrup.

She closed her eyes.

When she opened them he was watching her with puzzlement and faint concern.

"Are you all right?"

She shrugged and reached for the envelope. Her hand trembled, and he intercepted it.

His hand was as strong and warm as she remembered it from yesterday's brief handshake. But now she could also feel the exchange of energy as if he was pouring strength and confidence into her.

Which, of course, was ridiculous. He had no confidence in her whatsoever!

She met his eyes with surprise.

He let go of her hand as if it was hot. "Are you all right?" he repeated. He picked up a cookie, as if he needed to do something with that hand now that he found it empty.

"I guess," she murmured. "Sometimes what I find isn't very pleasant."

His brows lowered and he searched her face.

Looking, she guessed, for the lie, thinking it was part of her act. Weeping and wailing and gnashing of teeth.

She drew in a deep breath, composing herself. She wanted to get this over with. She wanted him and his enticing masculine scent and his insulting disbelief out of her house.

She opened the envelope and carefully slid the contents onto her kitchen table. A slender gold wristwatch, a school ring and a medallion on a chain lay before her.

She glanced at him. His face was closed. He was going to tell her nothing about the objects, give her no clues, allow no room for interpretation or intuition. She didn't tell him she preferred it that way.

Slowly, having to force herself, she picked up the ring. Her relief was almost instant. She closed her eyes, allowing herself to feel the warmth coming from the ring.

"I feel vitality," she said after a long time, "energy. Youthful energy. I see long, blond hair and long legs, like a spring filly. I see her jumping higher and higher. Yelling, calling out encouragement."

Hawk stared at her, flabbergasted. She sat across from him, looking extremely tranquil, serene, her voice soft but sure and confident.

She was holding Samantha, the cheerleader's, ring. He fought back his initial reaction of astonishment. This was, then, how easy it was to fool people. Logically, if he thought about it, which he intended to do, there were lots of ways she could know. Who had she talked to since yesterday? It was a small town. By now, lots of people must know the girl was gone.

He selected another cookie, as if it would anchor him to the real world.

"I see trees and water. She's very much alive. She's in love."

His cynicism was intact, like a comforting wall that he was on the other side of. Yeah, right, he told her silently. Over two thousand lakes in Idaho and she sees water. Big deal.

"I see a green truck," she said. "An old truck, very old, those big round fenders and narrow tires."

He frowned. He'd seen a truck like that around town from time to time. Of course, no doubt she had, too.

She opened her eyes and set the ring down. "That's all I get."

Again he noticed her hesitation before she picked up the next item, Sadie's watch. She was either a damn good actress or her fear was real—her fear that she could sense tragedy through the personal possessions of strangers.

Her eyes closed again, and she stroked the watch lightly with neatly manicured fingertips. For a long time she didn't speak.

The cookies were wonderful, chewy and loaded with chocolate chips. He hadn't had a cookie that didn't come from a bag in about ten years. He didn't want to make a pig of himself, but her eyes were closed, anyway. He slid another one off the plate.

"I sense struggle here. Sadness. But a strong spirit. This girl will go far."

He realized he actually felt relieved that she thought Sadie wasn't dead, either. Then he realized he was being sucked in, despite that high wall of cynicism he stood behind. It probably had something to do with the cookies. Kate Shea was no more aware of whether Sadie was alive than he was.

"Smoke," she said softly. "Loud noises. She's tired. A sign flashing. It says Giorgio's. And the green truck. I see the truck again."

She held the watch for a while longer, looking troubled, but then set it down.

She picked up the medal and chain.

Now, he thought, this is where it gets interesting. The chain was a Saint Christopher's medal that he had worn as a boy. He hadn't worn it since entering the academy.

He was about to find out what a faker she was. Though looking at her, he couldn't quite make himself believe she was an intentional faker. She'd probably talked herself into believing all this hogwash.

She picked up the chain, closed her eyes, dropped the chain and medal from hand to hand.

"It's very cold," she said slowly. "The boy is dead."

It was everything he could do to keep from snorting. But then he wondered how she knew it was a male, when he'd told her only about females in the case.

"I see him standing on a dock. His back is to me. He's fishing. Fly-fishing."

Hawk could feel the blood draining from his face. As a boy, almost every moment of every summer had been spent on his grandpa's dock, at a cabin not far from here, the fly-fishing rod in his hands, the rainbow trout jumping high in the lake. It was that cabin, her happy memories of summers spent in Idaho, that had made his sister choose to relocate to Sleepy Grove.

"His back is to me, but I feel his...contentment. He is happy. Oh, how this boy laughs. He is so alive. So alert to his world—the woods and the smells and the fish...and the way the light looks on the water and feels on his skin. He is full of wonder." She frowned suddenly. "Not dead," she whispered. "I made a mistake. Lost. This boy became lost within the man he became."

Kate opened her eyes suddenly. "I'm sorry," she said, "one of the parents must have given you the chain by accident. It doesn't belong to a girl."

She dropped it on the table as if it was hot, looked at him and then looked swiftly away. He hoped he didn't look as sheepish as he felt.

"I don't know if any of that helps you."

"I don't know, either," he said, eyeing her warily. Did she guess the chain was his? How far did her intuition go? That must be what it was. Still, the chain was masculine. It wouldn't take much of a reach to guess it belonged to a boy, rather than a girl. It was quite possible she had just taken a wild stab in the dark. After all, childhoods didn't vary that much from kid to kid, did they?

He looked at her sharply. She looked tired and pale, but relieved.

"Have you done much of this?" he asked, sipping his tea.

"As little as I can," she answered back with a wan smile. "It was okay this time."

"But it isn't always?"

"No."

He heard a flatness in her reply that he recognized. The same flatness that came into his tone when someone probed something that was too hard to remember, too terrible to talk about.

She had secret places, he realized, as deep as his.

She didn't seem at all offended. "You probably know as much as me about how this works."

"Oh."

"Have you ever been in danger?" she asked him.

"Yeah. Once or twice."

"Have you ever had the hackles rise on the back of your neck? Have you ever known you were in trouble a split second before you were?"

He was staring at her. He knew that feeling, all right. It had saved his life more than once, that deep intuition of *something*. He nodded reluctantly.

"That's how it works. Exactly like that. Science can't measure it, logic can't explain it, but that doesn't make it any less real."

Her eyes were very dark, looking more gold than green.

Hawk had the strangest sensation of danger right now. Eyes like those could be very dangerous to a man.

"Thank you very much," he said abruptly, scooping up the ring and the watch and the chain and shoving them back in the envelope. "I'm sorry to take so much of your time. Just send the chief a bill."

A fiendish little grin danced across her features and washed away that weary look. "I don't charge for this," she said sweetly. "It would be like charging to say a prayer for someone."

"Well, there are people who do that."

Her grin died. "I hope I don't look like one of them."

"The problem is they always look just like everybody else. It would sure make my job a lot easier if they didn't."

He could tell he was losing ground fast. Women didn't appreciate being told they looked like everybody else, especially when the "everybody else" he was referring to was a slightly unsavory element.

Still, he also knew he was glad he was losing ground.

There was something very compelling about Katie Shea.

She'd probably put a spell on him, put a potion in his tea, added more than chocolate chips to those cookies he'd eaten so many of.

He backed away from her. How many of those cookies had he eaten? Half a dozen? He'd probably be baying at the moon by midnight. Or seeing her eyes long after his were closed. "See you around sometime," he said with a total lack of sincerity.

She didn't reply. She was still sitting at the table, not even looking at him, but looking out her back window, a funny expression on her face.

It wasn't until he got into his car that he realized how long it had been since he had laughed like that boy who'd stood on the dock below his grandfather's cabin.

And realized how much he missed that lost part of himself.

Katie sat at the kitchen table for a long time after he was gone, thinking not of him and not of the girls he had come asking about.

She was thinking of that boy on the dock.

She had felt the oddest sense of connection with him. She wished he had turned around so she could have seen his face.

She felt as though he would be somebody she knew and loved deeply. Or could love deeply.

For a split second she had felt as if her soul had merged with his. As though she had felt what he was feeling in those moments, felt his deep peace with his world, his oneness with it, his aliveness.

But she reminded herself the boy was gone. Lost within an unknown man.

A man who had become a banker or a lawyer or a shoe store salesman. One of those girls' brothers or fathers. He might be somebody she saw every day.

It left her with an unsettled feeling she didn't fully comprehend or like.

Impatient with herself, she got up and cleared the tea things and the cookies from her table.

His tea was virtually untouched, but she had to smile when she saw how many cookies he'd devoured. Did she make him as nervous as he made her? Or was it the unfamiliar ground they had crossed into?

He didn't seem a man given to nerves. He'd probably just been hungry. Perhaps the man was starving. He didn't look like the type who'd be able to do much more than open a can of wieners and beans for himself.

Too bad she hadn't had any eye of newt to exchange for the chocolate chips.

Hawk lay on his couch, shirtless, his crumpled uniform shirt on the floor beside him. He flipped through the Yellow Pages, keeping one eye on the ball game. A TV dinner congealed in its tray on the coffee table. The open can of root beer beside it left a new sticky ring every time he picked it up.

Bars. Restaurants. What else would have a flashing sign that said Giorgio's? She had said the sign was flashing, hadn't she? He felt a little silly for even looking, but on the other hand he had no place else to turn in this case.

He'd spent the better part of a week talking to people, over and over again. Parents. Family. Friends. He was getting nowhere. He had a feeling there were things that the parents of Samantha, the cheerleader, weren't telling him.

He sighed. There was nothing in the Sleepy Grove and District phone book. Tomorrow he'd check the library phone books. And if there was nothing there, would he be relieved or sorry?

He'd driven by Kate Shea's place twice in the past week. He told himself he was just in the neighborhood, but deep down inside he knew he was hoping for another glimpse of her legs or the lacy top of that camisole. Deep down inside he was hoping she'd be working in her front flower beds, turn and see him, wave, invite him in for cookies.

Give him the satisfaction of saying no, of proving to himself he was not caught in the spell of her eyes—or her cookies.

His phone rang before he had to answer that question.

He unfolded himself from the couch and went into the tiny compartment that passed for a kitchen. He picked up the phone, casting a jaundiced eye around his place. It looked about as homey as an interrogation room.

A nice watercolor and a new couch might do the trick.

"Hi, Mary," he greeted his sister. "Yeah, just watching the ball game. No. I don't have a date.... Yes, I know it's Friday night.... For God's sake, Mary, I'm thirty-seven years old. I don't need a date on Friday night to make my life complete. Some chocolate chip cookies would probably do it.

"You'll make me some? Hey, thanks, Sis... No, I don't have a date for tomorrow, either... No, I don't plan on getting one.... You wonder if *what?*... No! I should have known you wouldn't make me cookies out of the goodness of your heart.... What do you mean it's only a baby?"

His sister and her husband Jack wanted to go to a play in Coeur d'Alene the following night. Their regular baby-sitter had just called in sick. Mary was nervous about trying somebody new when they'd be out of town.

"*I'd* be somebody new," he protested.

"Nonsense. You're her uncle. She loves you."

He was not quite sure how his sister had reached that conclusion. He had held the baby, Brittany, exactly once. She had burped up on him. Was that how babies demonstrated their fondness?

"Mary, I can't. I don't know anything about babies. . . . She'll be sleeping? What if she wakes up?"

He realized he'd moved from a definite "no" to "what if." His sister, no dummy, realized it, too.

"We've had these tickets for over a month. We hardly get out at all. We need to spend some time together."

"You're together all the time."

"*Alone* together. Without a baby and bottles and diapers."

"Diapers," he repeated. "Look, Mary—"

"I'll make you a year's supply of cookies."

"I can't change diapers."

"She'll be sleeping! Besides, you're a big, tough cop. What could a dirty diaper do to you?"

His reaction could ruin his reputation as a big, tough cop. Then he thought about having his freezer packed with cookies. He'd never again have to think of those melt-in-your-mouth ones that Katie Shea had made.

"A year's supply of cookies, and—"

"Anything."

"I need some help picking out some new furniture."

There was a long silence on the end of the phone. "Hawk?"

"What?"

"Are you sure you haven't met a woman?"

Chapter Three

Mary and Jack's place was just a few blocks from Kate Shea's. As in most towns, the homes got progressively newer and larger as they got farther from the town's core.

Mary and Jack's was an ultramodern California-style home with arched windows, deep carpets and more square footage than a family of twenty-two could have reasonably enjoyed.

They had the biggest TV set he had ever seen, Hawk thought contentedly as he tried out their channel changer from his resting place in the deep folds of their leather couch.

Mary had left written instructions—the folder that sat on her dining room table was thick enough that it might have contained the operations manual for a battleship. None of which he was going to need, because his darling niece was fast asleep in her pastel-colored nursery, her fanny in the air and her thumb in her mouth.

He had peeked in on her, upon arrival, and said a little prayer over her, something to the effect that if she didn't sleep for at least the six or seven hours her parents were going to be gone, he wouldn't get her a shiny red Corvette for her eighteenth birthday.

Mary had also left out several decorating magazines, her eyes glinting with an enthusiasm that made him slightly uneasy.

He flipped through one called *New Mexican Magic*. He noticed there wasn't any mention of price. He wasn't sure if what he'd meant when he'd talked about getting some furniture went as far as terra-cotta tiles and vases full of dried weeds.

The television had a hundred and twenty-two channels, and he couldn't find a single thing to watch.

He made popcorn in the microwave, scorching it only slightly, and debated adding a microwave to the furnishings he wanted. He'd rather have a microwave than an Aztec weaving.

He put the TV on the country music station and skimmed through the rest of the magazines. None of them gave him the feeling he wanted.

The exact feeling he'd experienced when he'd walked into Katie Shea's living room.

Maybe he'd just buy a yellow couch like hers. She'd never be at his house. How would she know he was a copycat?

He'd spent his day off, today, at the library looking through all the Idaho State telephone directories. Then he'd started on Montana. The librarian he'd had dinner with at Bill and Wilma's had been there, looking daggers at him because he'd never called her.

How could he tell her she was better off without him? Maybe he'd invite her over to his place. The decor would probably give her the general idea.

He'd read telephone books until his eyes blurred. He couldn't find a place called Giorgio's. Big surprise.

The magazines slipped off his chest onto the floor. In the background Big Joe Jeepers crooned about the coon dog he still missed twenty-six years after he'd buried it under the sycamore in his backyard.

Hawk remembered the dog that had accompanied him through the days of his youth, a long-haired shepherd he'd very originally called Rex.

He felt a lump in his throat, and felt irrationally angry with Kate Shea. Why had she brought him back to those lazy days on his grandfather's dock?

His eyes closed. He remembered what the sun felt like on his cheeks, the quickening excitement of having a tug on that line, the dog lying in the shade, snoozing and panting.

He had nearly drifted into dreams of hot and uncomplicated summer afternoons when he heard the first little peep.

His eyes shot open. "Please don't wake up," he whispered.

The next little peep was slightly more demanding than the first.

He jumped off the couch and raced to the instruction sheets on the dining room table.

There it was. "If the baby wakes up," he read, and she was definitely awake now, peeps having progressed to sobs, "there is a bottle of formula in the fridge. Heat in the microwave for thirty seconds—"

He was reading the instructions and feeling around in the fridge. Without taking his eyes off the instructions, trying to ignore the god-awful howls now emerging from the nursery, he pushed buttons on the microwave.

"Test to make sure it's not too hot."

He took the bottle out and stared at it. Grimacing, he put it to his lips and took a quick pull. Ghastly, but not too hot.

"Be sure to pick up the baby when you give her the bottle. A propped bottle is not safe."

Not safe. Pick up baby. He went up the stairs, two at a time, and burst into the nursery.

Brittany, standing inside her crib and holding tight to the top bar, fell silent, regarding him with shocked surprise.

"Hi," he said casually.

She screwed up her little face so tight her eyes closed.

"Don't do that. I brought you a bottle."

She let out a long, piercing wail that sent shivers up and down his spine.

"Alfred Hitchcock could have used a baby just like you," he said desperately. He went over and picked her up.

Her diaper was so soggy it soaked his arm.

He tried to put the bottle in her mouth. She smashed it with her little fist so ferociously that it flew out of his hand.

He stared at her, his heart beating as though he'd just run two miles after a mugger.

He rocked her awkwardly. Those little fists flailed, and her face was becoming a very unbecoming shade of purple.

Two hours later she was still screaming. The bottle was cold as ice and untouched. The diaper she had on was dry if not exactly secure, but he'd wrecked the stupid little plastic tabs on three of them before he'd gotten this one to stay on.

His skin was clammy. Seventeen years of police work that would have turned a lesser man to jelly, and this kid did it to him in two hours.

He plunked her back down in her crib and shut the door, standing outside of it breathing hard, not knowing what to do next. He *always* thought clearly in a crisis. He *always* knew what to do next.

And then it came to him. The pounding of his heart calmed. In his mind's eye he saw that photograph in Kate Shea's living room. He could picture every detail. The way her throat looked with her head thrown back, the way the sun caught in the red strands of her hair. The happy look on that baby's face as it tried to explore her nose. Kate Shea would know all about how to make a happy baby. He was sure of it.

He found her number in the phone book and dialed it without hesitating.

"Hello?" Her voice was sleepy, and for a minute he imagined what she looked like, sleep flushed and tousled. He wondered if she wore lace or flannel. He glanced guiltily at the clock. For God's sake, it was Saturday night. How was he supposed to know she'd be in bed already?

"Kate? It's me. Hawk Adams."

Silence greeted his announcement. Flannel, he decided. She was definitely a flannel type of lady.

"I was over there the other day—"

"I know who you are."

"Kate, I have an emergency on my hands. I need your help."

"What kind of an emergency?"

"You'll see when you get here." He gave her the address, before she had time to wake up and come to her senses, and hung up abruptly.

She barely knew him. Why would she come? It would be a stupid thing to do, to go to a strange house when a man you barely knew summoned you there.

Even if he was a cop.

But then this was Sleepy Grove, and she was the type of woman who left her door unlocked.

He hoped her trust would hold out for a little longer. Brittany's shrieking in the background was now scraping across his nerve endings, making him feel homicidal.

If Kate didn't come, then what?

But she came. The doorbell rang within five minutes, and she stood on the doorstep looking tousled and as wonderful as a guardian angel.

He resisted the impulse to plant a kiss on her cheek—still pink from sleep.

"Come in."

She stepped in cautiously and heard the baby. Her eyes flew to his face.

"My sister's," he told her. "Honestly, I have tried everything I know how. I can't make her stop."

A smile tugged at her lips. "It's not known to kill them."

"It was me I was worried about," he admitted. "Can you—"

She looked reluctant. She looked as if she wanted to do nothing more than step back out that door and pretend she didn't know him. But she didn't. She shrugged out of her coat and handed it to him.

Unless he was very mistaken, she had tugged a sweatshirt right over her pajamas. A little lace trim peeked beguilingly out of the vee at her neck. He didn't think they trimmed flannel pajamas in lace.

He hastily pulled his eyes back up to her face, that wholesome, reassuring, I'll-know-what-to-do-with-a-baby face. She followed the sound of the caterwauling without difficulty to the stairs and went up them.

He followed her, trying hard not to notice how her light blue jeans hugged her nicely—very nicely—rounded bottom. It was still that view that was distracting him when she bent and took the distressed baby from its crib. She had a certain sureness about her in the way she picked the child up.

"Could you warm me a bottle?" She turned and looked at him. Her eyes were huge, and her hair, which didn't look as if she'd taken the time to comb it, fell becomingly over one eye.

"Oh, sure. Thirty seconds." He dashed from the room.

While he was gone he noticed the wailing stopped. His ears rejoiced in the silence.

He went back up to the room, not-too-hot bottle in hand.

Kate had turned a lamp on and was sitting in a rocker, the baby tucked in tight to her breast. She was cooing to Brittany, talking to her so softly he couldn't hear what she was saying.

Not that it mattered. His niece, the she-devil, was looking up into Kate's face with sleepy adoration.

He handed Kate the bottle, and she took it without looking up at him. She waved her hand at him, dismissing him from the room as if he were a pesky fly.

He left, shutting the door behind him.

But he stood in the hall for a long time, listening to her funny voice as she sang the Big Joe Jeepers song about a long-dead dog.

After a while a blessed silence fell over the huge house. She came out of the room and started when she nearly bumped into him.

"Oh!" she said. "I thought you'd gone downstairs."

"You might have needed me."

She tried to smile. In the dim light of the hall, he saw she'd been crying.

He reached up and touched her wet cheek. "Kate?"

She brushed by him. "I have to go."

He couldn't let her. He reached out and grabbed her hand, spun her around.

She resisted for a moment, panic rising in her face. And then her soft, sweet curves were pressed into him and she was sobbing against his chest.

"Big Joe Jeepers has that effect on me, too," he said awkwardly, patting her back clumsily.

"Who?" she murmured into his chest. He could feel a big damp spot growing where she was crying on him. It didn't feel the same as the wet spot the baby had left on him. Not at all.

"The guy who sings the song about the dog."

"Oh."

He lifted her chin and looked down into her eyes. Green tonight. Murky green, as if they held a great deal of sorrow. Suddenly he knew she hadn't been crying about a dog.

Her pain made him want to hold her forever. And *forever* was about the scariest word in his vocabulary.

Of course, he of all people knew there was no such thing. He'd seen a folded flag or two handed to women too young to be burying their husbands.

He backed away from her. "Uh, can I make you a cup of coffee?"

"No, I—"

"Tea!" he said, remembering the concoction he'd been served at her place. "Tulip lips!" Did Mary keep tulip lip tea?

"Rose hips," she said, a tiny smile playing across her lips.

The smile made him want to hold her more than her tears had. The hall seemed very small, like her breasts were just inches from his chest. If he moved, just a bit—

"I really do have to go." She broke the spell of that physical closeness, going lightly down the stairs.

She really did have to go. No question about that, he told himself.

"What if she wakes up?" he heard himself asking.

"I don't think she will."

"Would you stay for a while? Just to make sure?"

She hesitated.

"I'll make some popcorn." *What the hell are you doing, Adams?*

She seemed to be wondering exactly the same thing. There was a huge question in her huge eyes, and it was not entirely without suspicion.

As if she thought he might have lured her over here to steal a few kisses or something.

Sure, lady, I was poking pins in the baby just to get you over here, because I haven't been able to get your lips out of my head for a week.

His eyes went to her lips. It was true. He hadn't.

"Have a seat," he said, gesturing at the big leather couch. He picked up the bowl of popcorn that was on the coffee table as casually as he could. "I'll be right back. Do you want some tea?"

"All right," she said, "if it's herb."

Herb, he repeated to himself. How had he managed to forget that? Miss Wholesome of Sleepy Grove was a certified quack.

So why had she been the first person he'd called to help him with Brittany? The only person he'd called?

She tucked her feet up under her and looked around the room with cautious interest.

That was the difference between a man and a woman, he thought, going into the kitchen. A man's eyes got as far as the channel changer.

He found another bag of that miracle popcorn and tossed it in the microwave, setting the time for a few seconds less than the last bag he'd cooked.

Mary had this aggravating habit of hiding all her appliances as if they were unbearable to look at, and after a long search he found her electric kettle. After a longer one, he found some loose tea bags, unlabeled, that smelled like they contained an illegal weed. He popped them into the kettle.

There was a funny singing inside him.

Lordy, Hawk, he asked himself, *what the hell are you up to?*

Katie wondered what on earth she was doing sitting here in this rich-looking room. She should have gone home. She heard a crash in the kitchen and debated going to help him.

No, she had helped Hawk Adams quite enough for one night. For some reason it was hard being in the same room with him.

That reason being that her heart did ridiculous things inside her chest. If Hawk had looked big and masculine in uniform, for some reason he looked even more so without it.

Tonight he was dressed in jeans faded nearly white. One knee was out of one of the legs. They hugged his flat fanny in a way that made her throat go dry. With the jeans, he wore one of those short-sleeved sport shirts that all men wear—navy blue, with a tiny manufacturer's emblem over his left breast. It's just that he didn't look like all men. The shirt molded the depth and strength of his chest, and showed off the powerful ripple of his arms most distressingly.

And what on earth had possessed her to fling herself against him and sob as though her heart had been broken?

She remembered the feel of that big chest on the receiving end of her crushed breasts and shivered. Had his eyes really trailed to her lips with such heat it had nearly scorched her?

And if they had, why was she sitting here calmly, waiting for him, instead of running for cover?

It had been a long time since she had been with a man. Was she getting desperate? Were her hormones going into full mutiny? Were they going to take over her mind soon?

He came in with the tea tray.

Very soon . . . the way her heart leapt.

Katie tried hard not to smile. He was walking very slowly, glaring down at the contents of the tray as if he dared anything to move unexpectedly.

Finally he made it to the coffee table and set things down with a relieved sigh. Looking very pleased with himself, he poured her a coffee mug of tea and then one for himself.

To her abject relief, he sat in the big leather chair across from her.

"Have you made any progress tracking down those missing girls?"

He shook his head and took a sip of his tea. His eyes nearly crossed.

Curious, she took a sip of her own. The gurgle of laughter started up her throat and prevented the tea from going down. She choked.

And before she knew it, he was over there slamming her on the back, making things much worse than they had to be.

"It's pretty horrible, isn't it?" he said, mercifully stopping thumping her on the back and unmercifully taking up residence right beside her on the couch.

His leg brushed hers. His thighs were as rock hard as she had known they would be.

"It's not exactly that it's awful," she said to him when she'd regained her breath. Moving out of contact with his leg, she took another small sip of the tea.

"It's awful."

"It's medicinal tea," she told him.

"Medicinal. For what?"

She hesitated, then smiled. "PMS."

"PMS," he repeated slowly as if he were saying some foreign language phrase, the meaning of which would come to him if he repeated it often enough. "PM—" The meaning obviously came to him, and she watched the tide of brick red move up the column of his throat.

He was different tonight. Not the same self-possessed, closed-off man who had visited her house twice.

The situation with the baby had brought his guard down. Way down. She suspected it was usually quite high. And now he'd embarrassed himself. She was oddly charmed by his embarrassment.

But he was only embarrassed for a moment. His lips began to twitch, and then he was laughing.

It was a deep laugh, wonderful-sounding, a sound she suspected he did not make often. She had been right about the dimple. It sliced deep into the firm plane of his cheek. She could not help but be caught up in the infectiousness of his laughter, and she laughed with him.

The laughter stopped as suddenly as it had begun, replaced by something even more magical.

Her eyes met his with awareness and with wonder.

He was gorgeous, especially when he let go like that. For a moment she was teased by a funny sense of déjà vu, but his hand, reaching tentatively toward her lips, stopped that feeling before it reached any kind of conclusion.

His index finger touched her lower lip with incredible tenderness. His eyes had darkened to a stormy shade of gray she had never seen before.

The hormones that had been threatening to mutiny took over the steering of her ship with damnable ease. She leaned toward him.

It was all the invitation he needed. His free hand tangled in the hair at the back of her neck, drawing her closer to him, and then his lips were on hers.

They stole her breath. They were hard and soft, cool and on fire at the same time.

She tasted him with an astounding lack of reserve. He tasted her back, his tongue touching her lips and her teeth and then gently exploring the contours of her mouth. If his mouth was gentle, the rest of him was sending off alarm signals of urgency. His hard body was pressing into hers. She could feel his strength, and it was a comforting strength. She could feel his desire, and it was not comforting.

It was downright dangerous.

She was a cautious woman. She had always been cautious. Reserved. Measuring each move before she made it, calculating the risks.

But not this time. His danger felt compelling, like going for a walk in an electrical storm—it invited life to course and sing through her veins. She felt as if she had never been alive before—just accepting a dim and dull replica of the real thing.

And those thoughts felt like a betrayal to all that she had loved before and lost!

She yanked away from him and leapt up off the couch.

"I'm sorry," she said distractedly.

He stood and took her shoulders. "There's nothing to be sorry for."

Something calmed within her as she stared up at him.

"Sit down," he said quietly. "Eat the popcorn. I'll make some more tea, if you want. Unless—" he slid her a mischievous look, and she couldn't help but laugh.

From tears to fear to laughter in the blink of an eye. She wondered how she must look to him. "Do I seem a little moody to you?"

"Nah," he disagreed. "You seem—" he sighed "—sexy as hell."

She stiffened. "I must go." She felt as though she couldn't play this game anymore. The man-woman game. She didn't understand the rules. She'd been married when the rules were changing. She'd been a mother.

Now men and women seemed to get to sex with alarming quickness. The few times she'd dated since the accident, she'd always found that the men had wanted too much too fast.

She wanted him not to be like them.

She wondered why. Hawk Adams had struck her from the first moment as being a cynical, hard man who'd seen just a little more than his fair share of the world's viciousness.

He hadn't shown any liking for her, or respect, either.

And here she was accepting his advances with enthusiasm that should be reserved for manna from heaven.

"I don't know what got into me," she said stiffly.

He looked as though he knew exactly what had gotten into her. Lust. But his face was wearing that cool, watchful mask that was more familiar to her.

She walked swiftly away from him, through to where her coat and shoes were.

She put them on hastily, not looking at him.

"Look, Kate, thanks for bailing me out. I really appreciate it."

She did look at him then. He was leaning his big shoulder against the doorjamb, his thumbs hooked through his belt loops. He made the kind of picture a woman could take and hang on her wall.

"Why did you call me?" she whispered.

"I don't know anybody else who knows anything about babies."

"And what made you think I knew anything about babies?"

"That picture over the bookcase in your living room."

"Oh." She looked away from him, eager to be into the coolness of the night, alone with her misery... and her memories.

"Whose baby was that?"

Her eyes clouded with tears again. She bit her lip. He tried to pull her close, but this time she pulled away.

"It was my baby," she said with dignity. "She died in a car accident. So did my husband. It was a drunk driver. At four o'clock in the afternoon."

"Kate." There was a stricken look in his eyes, as if he wanted desperately to take away the pain that, of course, no one could ever take away.

She reached for the doorknob, but his hand was resting on the door.

"When did it happen?"

"A long time ago. Six years."

"I'm so sorry."

She looked again, desperately, at the door. His hand still rested there. Of all the things she did not want from this man, she did not want his pity.

"Could we go out for dinner sometime?"

She pried his hand off the door. Was that pity talking? Or lust? Did it matter?

"Absolutely not," she said, yanked the door open and ran into the night, aware of thunder-gray eyes following her with an emotion she could not understand.

Chapter Four

Kate drove home, but when she pulled up in front of her house she felt unable to go in. She sat in her car for a moment, noticing her knuckles were white against the steering wheel, reflecting her tension. She abruptly released her hold and stepped out of the car, as if in doing so she could deny the turbulence within her.

Though the wind had risen and there were scattered drops of rain beginning to fall, when she glanced at the house, she realized her attempts at self-denial had not been successful and she could not go in. Shoving her hands deep in her jacket pockets, she put her head down against a chill wind and began to walk, trying to burn away some of the restless energy churning within her.

The houses along her street were dark. A car went by, but other than that Sleepy Grove was living up to its name. Sleeping.

She'd been here four years. She'd told people it was the reasonable price of real estate that had attracted her. She told people it was the small-town atmosphere and the low crime rate that had attracted her.

He would probably tell her it wasn't safe for a woman to walk alone at night. He was a strong man, the type who would try to impose his will on others, perhaps without even knowing he was doing so.

She had made the right decision, closing the door firmly on his invitation to get to know each other better. An invitation, she reminded herself, motivated by pity or lust, or a combination of both.

No, she did not need any complications in her life. It was a simple life, really. A large insurance settlement had guaranteed her comfort for the years to come. She had her small house and her garden. It was all very safe and tidy.

He would not be a safe man, or tidy, either. He'd said nothing about his past, but danger lurked in the unsettling gray of those eyes. In fact, he'd probably danced with danger most of his life. He was probably addicted to it.

Absolutely the wrong bet for a woman who had already been widowed once.

Even the remote possibility that she would ever have to go through it again made her shudder with terror.

But as the rain began to come down in earnest, she had to admit it was as though he already had his big foot in the door she was trying so hard to shut.

He represented the unknown, a threat to her carefully structured world. She had never been the adventurous type. She had always been easily contented with small pleasures.

Why was that smoldering look in his eyes haunting her? Why was the way his arms had felt around her making her ache? How light her heart had felt when they'd laughed together, how alive she had felt when the laughter died!

"You're acting like an adolescent," she admonished herself out loud, turning toward her home.

But as soon as she was in the door she knew it was not just him she'd been trying to outrun.

The baby. Holding that baby in her arms, she had ached with tenderness, remembered so vividly the soft, sweet weight and warmth of Carly.

She crossed slowly from her front door, not hanging up her coat, heedless of the little drips that ran off the hem. Hesitantly she turned on the small stained-glass lamp on her bookcase and reached for the photograph, taking it gently from the wall.

She stared at the picture and traced lovingly the line of Carly's round cheeks and dimpled chin. She remembered the lively squirming energy of her, her gurgling laughter, her attempts to say words, her first steps.

In truth she had come here to Sleepy Grove not because it was small and not because it was safe and not because of the price of real estate. For two years she had felt her loss so intensely she had thought she could not live. Two years of restless nights and wayward thoughts and regrets. Two years of not eating properly and crying every time she smelled baby powder.

She had come to Sleepy Grove to start anew, to leave the past behind her. She knew no one here who would remind her. No memories.

She thought she had succeeded. In a way she had. She had successfully stopped feeling by eradicating from her life anything that made her feel. She'd found comfort in numbness.

And then he'd come along, and she realized uncomfortably her feelings were not as much under control as she'd thought. He made her feel things. And he made her aware of something. There was a future, a great beckoning unknown that she'd managed to ignore while she puttered with her flowers and painted her house.

And for the first time in a long time she could look to it with a tiny quickening of excitement. Maybe it was okay not to know what tomorrow held.

The weight of that baby in her arms, the soft sweetness of it pressed into her breast, had made her feel a strange aching sadness at first, but now the sadness had passed, and something even more terrifying was in its place.

A feeling of the world being right, of things moving on, of life being pure and good.

Hope.

She felt hope. And it was not until she felt it that she realized she had been without it for a long time.

And that it threatened the world she had built, where she didn't love anyone because love had hurt her so badly.

She was aware of a deep yearning in her.

And an even deeper fear of that yearning.

If she ever loved so deeply again and lost, she would not survive.

And Hawk Adams was the wrong type of man to take that kind of gamble on. He did too dangerous a job. All right, so it was Sleepy Grove.

But she realized it wasn't his job she thought was dangerous.

It was something about him.

He'd been a bachelor too long. He wasn't settled. The wrong type of man to take a risk on.

Rebelliously, a little voice insisted on having the last word.

"Well, couldn't you just have an affair with him?"

Something inside her stomach clenched at the thought. For a moment she pictured herself lying naked beside him in a tangle of sheets, morning sun spilling over the bed and painting his carved muscles gold.

She snorted at herself.

What a picture that made. His muscular perfection, her round tummy and tiny wrinkles. Reality. She was not young and coltish anymore. Babies changed women's bodies, and while it was nothing to be ashamed of it, it didn't exactly inspire fantasies of wild love scenes, either.

These thoughts were so unlike her that she blushed even though she was alone.

And then she laughed at her pure foolishness.

She looked at the photograph again, this time looking at herself. She felt as if she was looking at a stranger. That laughter-filled young woman was gone. As gone as that boy she had seen on the dock in her vision.

She had done well to say no to Hawk Adams tonight. The evening had stirred things in her that were best left undisturbed.

And if she ignored that feeling of regret for long enough, she was sure it would go away.

She'd turned him down flat, Hawk told himself. It was a good thing, really. And it didn't bother him at all. In fact, he hardly ever gave it a moment's thought.

Of course, he was giving it a moment's thought now, and it had happened nearly two weeks ago. It had stung, mildly. He wished women knew how a man had to screw up his courage to ask her out. That was what hurt. That's why he thought about it from time to time.

He was sitting behind Marvin Becker's hedge in one of the black-and-whites with the radar on. It was a beautiful spring day, the sun hot where it came through his window and touched his arm and the side of his face.

He simply had too much time to think, he told himself, and not enough to think about. Living life on the edge had had its advantages. The drive to survive had a way of crowding out lesser thoughts.

The birds were near rioting in the hedge beside him, and a car hadn't come by in twenty minutes. He hated this assignment, and his mind drifted back to her rejection of him, despite his resolve not to think about it anymore.

When was the last time a woman had refused him? A long time ago. Though of course that begged the question When had he last given a woman an opportunity to refuse him?

They always wanted too much of him. It was as if they wanted him to be this romantic figure they had read about in books, to charge into their lives on his white steed and rescue them from ever being bored or unhappy again. They wanted to know where he was every minute and wanted to talk to him once a day on the phone.

He just wasn't interested. When he tried to explain it to his sister, she'd rolled her eyes and told him to stop dating girls with bleached-blond hair and breast implants.

Which he probably would have been insulted by if there wasn't a kernel of truth in there.

Suddenly he remembered being fourteen and asking Betty Smith to a school dance. She lived next door to him and was three years older. She could beat him at chess and arm wrestling, too. She'd been cute and real, and he'd loved her.

And she'd been very kind when she told him no.

He sighed. That was another thing about Kate Shea. He kept remembering these little fragments of a boyhood he'd thought was long forgotten. He kept remembering things about himself that now seemed to be lost.

At fourteen he'd asked Betty out with boldness, honest about who he was and what he'd been feeling, and fearless about sharing that with her.

He was not sure that he was capable of that anymore.

Not that it mattered of course. Not one little bit. It was really a blessing that Kate Shea had said no in such uncertain terms, and he knew it.

Besides, there was something pathetic about a thirty-seven-year-old man realizing he hadn't been in love since he was fourteen.

A car went by, and he was disgusted to see it was traveling just under the speed limit. Then he caught a glimpse of the driver, her nose tilted, her tousled hair auburn.

Her, he thought. And then he noticed that she had that car so packed with *something* that she had blocked her view out the back window.

He turned on the siren and pulled out behind her. Her car was a sturdy-looking, no-frills red sedan. Unlike the kind of women he'd dated, back when he'd still bothered, who had driven flashy sports cars or convertibles.

Hawk, he asked himself, *is this because she said no?*

Of course not, he told himself roughly, it was really for her own safety. He wouldn't give her a ticket, naturally, just a little warning, the same as he would do to any other citizen, driving under unsafe conditions. It would be worse if he *didn't* stop her, more of a betrayal to his badge and authority. That was his job. To protect and serve.

She pulled over, and he got out of his car, leaving the red and blues flashing. He was aware of her eyes, huge and hazel, watching him in her side mirror as he approached her.

Unless he was very much mistaken, her car was crammed to the roof with lilacs.

"Hello, Kate," he said coolly. "How are you?" He congratulated himself on his great policeman voice, deep and cool, indifferent. Not the voice of a man who was remembering the taste of her lips beneath his.

"Fine," she said, her voice as warm and golden as honey, "and you, Hawk?"

"Never been better," he said stonily, but he felt his indifference slip a notch at the way her eyes looked at him so damned directly. Wasn't she thinking of that kiss at all?

"The girls?"

He shook his head, his indifference slipping another notch. She cared about those girls. She wasn't so hot at hiding what she cared about—something like that boy he'd been a long time ago.

"Nothing, yet."

"I'm sorry," she said, and he could tell she really was. "How's Brittany?"

This was the problem with working in a small town, he thought. How was he supposed to be the voice of authority to someone who had witnessed the humiliating fact he was no match for a scrap of humanity that weighed in at about twenty pounds? Twenty-three with a soaking-wet diaper.

"Showing every sign of growing up to be a terrorist," he said grimly.

Kate laughed, and the sound was rich, like the spring afternoon all around him. It lit something in her eyes and made him aware that he wanted to make her laugh and often.

Which was a ridiculous thought to have about a woman so good at saying no. Not just no, he reminded himself. Absolutely not, no.

He got down to business, before he did something really foolish.

"Did you realize your vision is obstructed out your rear window?" He wanted to ask her where she was going with her car full of flowers, but decided it fitted right in there with tulip lip tea and reading fortunes. It was one of her little eccentricities. The ones he wanted to despise and instead was reluctantly intrigued by. Better not to know.

The scent of the flowers was hitting him now, honeyed and strong.

She didn't answer him, just continued to look at him, green eyes unwavering.

Of course she knew, he told himself.

"If you're transporting flowers again, perhaps you could make sure you don't block your view."

He sounded ridiculously formal and official. What was he becoming? There were people out there killing each other, and he was telling eccentric little ladies to watch the flower capacity of their vehicles.

She looked flustered. "You can give me a ticket, you know. If you want. If you're supposed to—"

He looked at her incredulously.

"I didn't mention Brittany to make you feel like you owed me something," she said, the color high in her cheeks, her freckles looking darker than they had the last time he had seen her.

It seemed like a very long time ago that he had thought she was some kind of charlatan.

"I know," he said. He wondered when he had last met anyone so completely without guile.

"Hawk, look," she whispered suddenly, and he saw her eyes glued to the side mirror.

He spun around, just in time to see an old green truck turning left and coming toward them.

He shot her a look and she nodded, her face suddenly pale.

Without hesitating, he stepped out in front of the truck, his left hand up, his right hand flagging the driver over to the curb.

The truck lumbered to a halt in front of her car.

"Stay here," he told her.

He was aware he had no reason to stop the truck, and he scanned it quickly. He noticed the license was bolted only on one side and about to come off.

He stepped up to the driver's-side window, all his senses on red alert, aware of Kate, aware of a need to protect her if things started to go wrong.

He eyed the youth in the driver's seat icily. He had long dark hair, and an earring dangled from one ear. He wore a faded jean jacket. But the interior of the truck smelled of old leather, well cared for, not booze or smoke.

"You're about to lose your license plate," Hawk said casually, sizing up the driver. He didn't mention it was the back one. He wouldn't have been able to see the back one at the time he'd flagged him over.

He was a good-looking boy, maybe eighteen or nineteen. He was looking at Hawk with bold dislike.

"Geez," he said to Hawk, "you're not going to give the Lilac Lady a ticket are you?"

He said this as if it would rate right up there with giving a ticket to Santa Claus.

"You know her?" Hawk snapped. Had he been watching her? Would Kate be the next to disappear?

He forced himself to relax. He couldn't start treating a vision as if it was a statement of fact. He was being ridiculous, anyway. Kate had nothing in common with the girls missing. She was probably a dozen years older than them. She was not blond, she did not have blue eyes, her name did not begin with the letters *Sa*. She probably wouldn't even be attractive to this young buck.

So why did he feel like a grizzly bear about to defend his territory?

The boy shrugged. "I've just heard of her."

"Where?" Hawk demanded softly.

The boy sighed and rolled his eyes. "She brought my great-aunt McGee some flowers last year, all right?"

McGee. Hawk felt his blood quicken, but he forced himself to go slow. "Why did she do that?"

"That's what she does," the youth informed Hawk. "She brings people flowers out of her yard. Old people. Shut-ins. The nursing home."

Hawk carefully schooled his features not to register the blow. Everybody in town, including this little thug, knew she was delivering flowers to shut-ins. And he'd pulled her over.

Way to go, Romeo, he told himself.

"And what do you do?" he asked the kid.

"Do you have a reason to be asking these questions?"

The bad ones always knew their rights, inside out and backward.

"Do you know Sadie McGee?" he asked abruptly, watching the boy's face closely.

He saw the shutters come down over those intelligent blue eyes.

"Sure," the boy said cautiously. "She's my half sister."

"Do you know where she is?"

"What's it to you?"

"A missing persons report has been filed on her."

"If she wanted people to know where she was, she'd tell them."

Hawk didn't like the answer. The boy seemed suddenly hard and tough, not just another maturing male battling his testosterone levels, looking for another bull to ram up against.

"Do you know where she is?" Hawk asked again.

"No," the boy said tersely, but Hawk knew it was a lie.

"Do you know Samantha Height?" he asked.

"No," the boy said, too quickly. Another lie.

Hawk held his gaze just long enough to let him know he knew it was a lie and then stepped back from the truck. "Get that license plate fixed," he suggested, his tone deliberately flat. But he saw the warning in his eyes register in the boy's own eyes. The boy gave him a vile look and drove away.

Hawk turned around. The Lilac Lady, Saint Kate, had gotten out of her car and was trying to rearrange the flowers so that she could see.

"Don't worry about it this time," he told her gruffly.

"I wanted to have an excuse to get a better look at him."

"And did you?"

She nodded.

"And?"

She smiled. "I got a good feeling from him. But I can't begin to tell you if that's premonition or intuition."

"He lied to me," Hawk said evenly.

"About what?"

"He said he didn't know where Sadie was, and I think he did. He said he didn't know Samantha at all, but I think he did."

"I thought you didn't believe in hocus-pocus," she said.

She was standing in the sun now, leaning up against her car, her arms folded casually over her chest. She was dressed in a tailored suit, pink, maybe silk. Despite one intriguing inch of her camisole showing, it was the type of outfit a woman wore to church.

He didn't go out with that kind of woman, anyway, he told himself.

"What do you mean about hocus-pocus?"

"I get feelings and they're hocus-pocus," she teased, "you get them and they're legitimate leads."

She was trying to tell him that his gut feeling, which he'd relied on for years, was the same as reading tea bags.

Holding objects and getting feelings from them. Fat chance.

"He may know something," she said, looking after the green truck, "but that boy didn't hurt those girls."

"You'd be surprised how much like a choirboy a serial murderer can look," he informed her grimly.

"If he was a killer, he certainly could have run you down. It was very dangerous how you stepped out in front of him like that."

Hawk laughed. "You don't know the meaning of the word."

"No," she said, regarding him thoughtfully, "I suppose I don't."

Lots of people asked him probing and personal questions about danger and his work. He was thankful she didn't, despite the opening he'd rather stupidly left her.

But something in the way she was looking at him made him think he wasn't quite the expert on danger that he thought he was.

"I should go," she said suddenly, as if she too was aware of a sudden sizzling change in the air around them. "The bouquets won't last long out of water."

The bouquets she was delivering to the town's shut-ins.

"That's a nice thing you do," he said gruffly.

"Oh." Her cheeks turned as pink as her jacket. "It's nothing, really."

But it was. Really. He watched her get in her car and drive away, the scent of lilacs drifting away with her.

He stopped at the library next. The librarian looked more like a *Cosmo* girl than ever, her lips and fingernails an astounding siren red.

He debated asking her out. It was as good as guaranteed that she wouldn't tell him "absolutely not" in a prissy little schoolmarm voice. He was willing to bet that powder blue sports car in the parking lot was hers.

But somehow his heart wasn't into asking her out.

He didn't have a heart, he reminded himself. But if he didn't, *something* was fluttering around damned uncomfortably every time he had a run-in with Kate Shea.

"Could I take a couple of the Washington directories home with me?"

He wasn't at all sure why she said yes, but she did, and he found himself on his couch that night going through yet more directories.

"Police work," he said, addressing the imaginary meeting of the Sleepy Grove Boy Scouts, "is basically very boring."

At nine o'clock, sitting among the clutter of discarded phone books, take-out pizza cartons, empty pop cans and some of the crumbs of the cookies he'd taken from his stash in the freezer, he found it.

What was as astonishing as finding it was that sometime, somewhere he had actually started to believe he would find it.

Because of that truck this afternoon? Anyway, there it was—Giorgio's Bar and Grill in Spokane. No display ad, just one line of black. He stared at it for a long time.

He dialed the number.

"Is Sadie there?" he asked. The background noise was very loud. He could hear glasses rattling and the dull roar of voices in the background.

"Sadie," somebody yelled. "Is there a Sadie here?"

He cursed his stupidity. Her brother had implied she didn't want to be found. If she was there, now she knew someone was looking. What was she running from?

Was he being ridiculous treating that woman's premonitions as if they were fact?

He slammed down the phone and dialed Kate's number. Somehow he remembered her number, as if his subconscious had debated dialing it again and again.

"Hawk Adams here," he said brusquely, when she answered. "I called about the case." Just to let her know, right off the bat, it was nothing personal.

"There's a place called Giorgio's in Spokane. I want to go see if she's there."

"That's a good idea." He could hear the uncertainty in her voice, the question she was too polite to ask.

"I want you to come with me," he said grimly.

He was prepared for her to argue, and he was already shaping his rebuttal in his head. Saying to her, "Look, lady, it's your vision, stand behind it."

So he wasn't quite prepared when she said, "All right, Hawk. I'll come. When?"

"Tomorrow," he said, and named a time. He hung up the phone. Suddenly he felt cold all over.

What was he doing? Using police work to get a date with a lady who didn't want to have a date with him?

His life was always nice and neat. Always. Everything in neat, tidy compartments, nothing out of place.

And that's how he wanted it.

The phone rang. He hoped it was her phoning to cancel.

Instead it was his sister's voice on the other end of the line.

"Hawk, Jack's mom just called. His dad has had a heart attack. We're flying to Florida tonight."

His sister enjoyed an astoundingly good relationship with her in-laws, and he could hear the pain and terror in her voice.

"I'm sorry to hear that, Mar. I'll keep an eye on the house for you."

"Actually, Hawk, I was going to ask you to keep an eye on something else."

"Sure."

"Brittany."

"Mary!"

"Hawk," she began, the control in her voice slipping, "we'll be at the hospital."

He wanted to tell her she wasn't thinking straight, which of course she was not. But then he'd dealt with people confronting crises all of his adult life, and that was a given. They didn't think straight.

"You're on your three days off, aren't you?"

For someone who wasn't thinking straight, she had his schedule down pretty good. He could hear the pleading in her voice. His sister really didn't ask him for much. She gave him a lot, but didn't ask for much back.

He thought of her trying to be there for Jack and his mother and the sick father, and trying to juggle the demands of the baby all at the same time. He thought of how she had told him Brittany's ears hurt from flying at Christmas.

He wasn't great at the big brother thing. Or the uncle thing, either.

But maybe he didn't have to be great at it. Just there.

"I'll come right over, Mary."

"Thank you," she said, her voice quavering uncontrollably.

And that's how, when he arrived at Kate Shea's the next morning, Brittany happened to be strapped securely into her baby seat on the bench seat beside him.

Kate came down the walk toward his vehicle. She had wondered if he would drive something low-slung and sporty and was relieved to see it was one of those crosses between a truck and a station wagon.

She'd been waiting for him, had not wanted him to get out and come up to her door.

She would have felt too much like a teenager going on a date.

Since seeing him yesterday she had not succeeded at all in quelling the feeling of regret she'd had about turning down his dinner date invitation.

And here she was going out with him, anyway. Professionally, of course, though she'd been nagged by a feeling that things that were meant to be always found a way.

Though it would be foolish to think anything was meant to be between her and that big, self-assured cop. He just reeked of confidence, of sureness. He had opened his vehicle door, and seeing her coming, just stood leaning on the hood of the truck, watching her with what seemed to be rather frank male appreciation.

As if he hadn't noticed the roundness at her tummy or the wrinkles around her eyes.

She had looked at herself for an extra-long time in the mirror this morning trying to decide if she had gotten it right.

What was right? She wanted to look casual. Unavailable somehow. *As if she didn't care.*

She had chosen a pair of taupe-colored jeans, a navy blue silk blouse and a paisley vest that picked up both colors. Understated. Cool.

They'd been thrown together to do a job. Even if he didn't respect her as a professional, and even though she had never thought of her unsettling gift in those terms, that was what she wanted to project. Cool professionalism.

As soon as she caught sight of the baby on the front seat, she knew she was doomed.

For a minute she had to struggle with blind panic, the same as when he had opened his sister's door to her the other night and she had heard the squalling of the baby.

At first, she just wanted to run back down her walk.

Then she felt angry. Did he know what babies did to women, especially a woman who had lost one? Was he so despicable he'd use his niece to try to win her affections?

Affections. Ha. A man like Hawk didn't want the affections of a woman like her.

So what did she think he wanted?

If he wanted a roll in the hay, she was sure he could do much better than a worn-out widow with gardening dirt under her fingernails and freckles across her nose.

Stiff with uncertainty, she regarded him across the top of the jade green truck. He was wearing a shirt a shade bluer than the bright spring sky. It was short-sleeved, showing off the round bulge of perfect biceps and a tan that hadn't come from a salon.

Closer, she could see he had a wrinkle or two fanning out from his own eyes. They did nothing to alter his attractiveness. Still, there was weariness in his face, faint dark crescents under those devastating gray eyes.

"We've had a family emergency," he said. "My sister's father-in-law is quite ill. They left for Florida last night."

"I'm sorry to hear that," Kate said, aware her voice sounded like it was coming from a long way away. She wanted so desperately to despise him. But rather than using his niece, he had stepped in to help in a family emergency, taking on something he really was in no way qualified or prepared to take on.

The sudden softness she felt for him was very threatening. She could, of course, plead illness and march back up the walk in her perfectly professional outfit. She could and she should.

But she didn't. She opened the door and slid into the seat.

The baby was strapped into the center position, and her baby smell filled the space.

Kate looked at her and couldn't help but smile. Her head was nodding, her chin on her chest, slobber pooling on the front of her little blue dress. Unless Kate missed her guess the dress was on backward.

Hawk slid into the vehicle. His jeans were soft with age and clung to his hard thigh muscles.

This was going to be impossible, she thought, closing her eyes briefly. She opened them just in time to see him give his niece a tortured look.

"If she sleeps now, is she going to be awake all night?"

"Again?" Kate asked gently, suddenly relieved for the baby between them, relieved that her mind had something to focus on other than his hard angles.

He grinned wearily. "Again."

"You could have called."

"Yeah. Well."

The memory of the last time he had called hung uncomfortably in the air between them.

"She's a beautiful baby, Hawk."

He looked pleased, though he responded gruffly, "I kind of like her . . . when she's sleeping."

Somehow Kate found herself reaching out and stroking the little pink hand. The baby reached out in her sleep and grabbed her finger, her hand closing around it tightly.

Oh no, Kate thought, battling the rising emotion in her throat. *I'm going to cry.*

Hawk apparently hadn't noticed. With a quick over-the-shoulder check he had pulled out into the street and was driving with a certain confidence and ease all her years behind the wheel had never given her.

"Could you tell me," he said, slipping a pair of sunglasses off the dash and onto his nose, looking straight ahead, "what you know about baby poop?"

The inclination to cry was gone, just like that. She gazed at him, wondering if he had done it on purpose, but his face gave away nothing. His tone indicated he was a scientist probing mysteries he didn't understand, nothing more.

She started to laugh. When he turned to her, his eyes hidden behind those glasses but his mouth turned down in a firm line, she forced herself to stop.

"Baby poop," she said obediently, and told him everything she knew.

Chapter Five

The baby peeped just outside of Spokane. Kate had to bite back laughter at the look of blind terror that crossed Hawk's handsome features as he cast an apprehensive glance at his niece.

Brittany sighed and blew a few bubbles. She struggled to open her eyes, but then her tiny shoulders relaxed again.

Out of the corner of her eye, Kate watched the tension in Hawk's big shoulders relax in unison with his niece's. Just when he had fully returned his attention to the road, the baby let loose an ear-piercing wail.

His face suddenly set in grim lines, his hands taut on the wheel, Hawk cut through two lanes of traffic to pull over on the side of the road.

By now it was everything Kate could do to keep the laughter inside her. The man, who had probably dealt with emergencies all his adult life, was acting worse than an about-to-be-father on the way to the hospital.

"Baby bag," he commanded tersely over the wails of his niece, who now had her eyes scrunched tightly shut and was flailing away with all four limbs. Hawk slammed the vehicle into neutral, undoing his seat belt. He reached into the back seat and retrieved a huge bag that looked suspiciously like a men's gym bag.

When he opened it, Kate could contain herself no longer. The bag was packed absolutely full. In one quick glimpse she spotted an entire sack of disposal diapers, two tubs full of wet wipes, at least a dozen bottles of formula, three rattles, one squeeze toy, a stack of sleepers and a sunbonnet.

"Is...this...all...for...today?" she managed to choke out.

At his grim nod, she could no longer contain the first squeak of laughter.

When he glared at her in baleful warning, she really started to laugh.

"I can't bear this racket," he called over the baby's howling. "I'm warning you, I can't."

That made her laugh harder. What did a "warning" from a big, tough cop mean? Tickets to follow?

Kate tried to stop laughing and couldn't. Instead she fumbled with the buckles on the baby seat and lifted Brittany into her arms.

The dress was indeed on backward. Kate laughed harder. The tears were coming down her cheeks. Her stomach hurt. She had been a girl, the last time she had laughed with such wild abandon, with such reckless enjoyment.

Even the baby stopped crying, looking at Kate with wide-eyed amazement. Then she smiled tentatively, cooed, wrapped a fist around Kate's hair.

Kate hugged her tight to her. The rush of laughter slowed and then stopped. She waited for the sadness, the feeling of loss, but it didn't come. Instead, as she looked back into the baby's eyes, she felt a most lovely tide of warmth creeping into her.

She heard a sound, oddly like a groan, and turned startled eyes to Hawk. For a strange, suspended moment she had almost forgotten his big presence in the truck.

He was staring at them, the tension gone from his face, a look she could not define replacing it. Tenderness? Something more, even deeper. A man who felt deep regret, who had missed something...

A moment later she was sure she was mistaken, that she had let her own imagination fill in the mystery that had been in those gray eyes for but a second.

His face closed down to its normal remoteness, and he uttered a single curse word. He got out of the car and slammed the door, hard.

Ignoring his big form, circling around the vehicle like a restless wolf, Kate rummaged around in the bag and found an insulated bag that contained yet more bottles and one large man's sock, clean, thank goodness. She took out a bottle, still warm, and tested it on her wrist.

She popped it into the baby's mouth, and Brittany sucked with greedy contentment, her eyes wide and unblinking on Kate's face.

She had gray eyes, just like her uncle's, light gray flecked with darker gray.

Kate talked to her in a low, soft voice. "Mommy's gone to be with Grandpa for a little while," she told her. Out of the corner of her eye, she could see Hawk over her right shoulder. He gave the rear tire a vicious kick.

"Uncle Hawk is very afraid of you, and you must try not to use that against him."

After several more tire kicks Hawk got back in the car. "Not flat, after all," he said, as if he'd sworn because his tire was flat and not because something had momentarily pierced the hard armor around his heart.

"Do you want to hold her?" Kate asked.

"Uh, not really." But even as he said it, he reluctantly held out his arms, a man, Kate noted, who took his responsibilities seriously.

Kate passed the baby over to him. She really wanted to keep her herself, but if he was going to be in charge for a few days it was essential that he learn a few basics.

He glowered at the baby. "She's doing it already."

Sure enough the baby was scrunching up her face.

"I think she's just imitating you," Kate said.

This earned her a glower of her very own. Brittany's mouth opened and an ear-piercing wail came out.

He held her out at arm's length but Kate did not take her back.

"Relax," she coached him. "I think she feels your tension."

"I am not tense!" Seeing Kate was not going to take the baby back, he set her once again on his lap.

For a man who was not tense, the muscles in those well-formed arms were rippling alarmingly.

"Talk to her," Kate hinted.

"About what?" he asked irritably.

"Anything. It's just the sound of your voice she'll like, not the words."

"Are you trying to be a prizewinning hog caller at the local fair?" Hawk addressed Brittany.

Kate handed him the bottle. "Here."

He shoved the bottle in his niece's mouth, and they scowled at each other, the baby sucking furiously, her eyebrows drawn down in a frown that was identical to that of her uncle.

"You could try talking to her some more," Kate suggested.

Hawk looked blankly down at the baby. After a long time, he said, "So what about those Blue Jays?"

"Softly," Kate suggested, "try to keep that come-out-of-the-car-with-your-hands-up tone out of your voice."

He spared her a withering glance. "You don't care one whit about the Blue Jays, do you, little Miss Pig Caller?" But he said it gently, some of his love for his niece slipping past his guard.

Brittany took the bottle out of her mouth. "Oopa, mooma," she cooed at him, then stuck it back in and slurped some more.

"She talked to me," he told Kate with amazement.

"I believe she did," Kate agreed, and was startled by the sudden light that suffused his face. For a moment she was left almost breathless with the feeling that she knew something about him, knew him . . .

But he started talking again. "There's room in the world for pig callers," he informed his niece solemnly. "And who knows? Someday you might like baseball. I might even take you to a game or two. Maybe—" he was really warming to his subject now "—maybe you'll lose interest in hog calling—there are only so many ways to say *suey,* after all—and be the first woman to play professional ball. But you have to promise me one thing." He leaned very close to the baby's ear and whispered.

The baby removed the bottle and cooed sloppily at him, milk dribbling down her chin.

"Thatta girl," he said, wiping the milk away with his shirtsleeve despite the cargo of wipes he had packed.

"What did you make her promise?" Kate asked.

He hesitated. He did not take his eyes off the baby. "Never to be a cop."

She was startled. "Is it so awful?"

He looked away from his niece's face and out the window. "I could never be anything else. But you pay a price for it, and I don't want her to pay it."

"And what price is that?" Kate persisted.

"It's hard to put it in words, but something gets cold inside you. It makes it hard to care about other people."

It was a warning, pure and simple. Briefly she could see the loneliness behind that implacable mask of strength. But if he was lonely, he was lonely by his own choosing, and she would do well to remember that. Again she was bothered by that strange feeling of knowing something . . . but it eluded her.

Hawk was putting Brittany back in her seat. Awkwardly he manipulated her uncooperative little limbs through the shoulder straps and buckled her in tight.

"Don't even think you're going to ride in Auntie Kate's lap," he told her sternly. "It's not at all safe. You have to be in your baby seat when you're in the car."

Auntie Kate, Kate registered, and mulled it over thoughtfully. Uncle Hawk and Auntie Kate. She could feel a tide of color moving up her neck into her cheeks. The man had just told her, in the simplest terms possible, that he was a lone wolf. And yet . . . She looked swiftly out her window, before he could see that high color in her cheeks and figure out what had put it there.

They found the bar and grill with very little difficulty. It was more than evident that Hawk had no trouble finding his way around in larger centers. He handled the traffic and the noise with complete ease. Both were jangling Kate, now more used to the Sleepy Grove pace of life.

They were in a very old part of Spokane, in front of a three-story sandstone building. Giorgio's was on the main floor and boasted one very dirty window and a sad-looking sign blinking on and off over the door.

It did not look like the type of place one took babies, but Hawk was obviously not well versed in such matters. He pried the baby from her car seat, tucked her under his arm like a squirming football and headed for the door. Kate went after him.

It was dark inside and reeked of stale beer and old smoke. When her eyes adjusted to the gloom she saw the floor was covered in sawdust and peanut shells. Only one or two of the tables were occupied. Three tough-looking youths slouched at the pool table, cigarettes drooping from their mouths.

Kate wanted to get the baby and wait in the car, but Hawk was already striding across that room toward the bar. She had to rush to catch up to him.

When he arrived he pulled the baby out from under his arm and plunked her well-padded fanny down right on top of the bar.

Brittany looked around with interest.

With one arm holding the baby on the bar, he used the other to fish around in his pocket. He pulled out a photo to show to the bartender who was eyeing the baby with wary distaste.

"Have you ever seen this girl?" he asked bluntly.

The bartender looked at the picture. Even Kate, who had no experience in such matters, saw the hood come down over his eyes. They flicked briefly to the baby.

"Does that belong to her?" he asked.

Hawk hesitated, and Kate was suddenly aware he was very capable of telling a lie if he thought it would forward his cause. It made a shiver go up and down her spine.

She suddenly became aware of his eyes on her face and knew she had been very transparent. Brittany was grabbing wildly at some brightly colored stir sticks, and Kate went and removed her from the bar.

"No," Hawk said, "the baby isn't hers."

"Doesn't matter. I've never seen that girl before in my life."

Kate knew instinctively what had happened. Despite the baby, Hawk had too much authority. Even without a uniform, it was too obvious he was a cop. The bartender thought Sadie was in trouble.

Quickly she set the baby back down on the bar, fished in her purse for a pen and scrawled a quick note on a napkin. She passed it to the bartender.

He scanned it quickly, glanced at her, then shrugged and nodded. He went through a door to the back.

"What was that all about?"

"I asked him, if he knew Sadie, would he please just call her and tell her the Lilac Lady from Sleepy Grove was here and would like to see her."

"I thought you didn't know her."

"I don't."

Hawk snorted. "Oh, then that should work."

The bartender came back after a few minutes. "Have a seat," he said gruffly.

Five minutes later the door squeaked open and Hawk recognized Sadie McGee standing there, looking around with a faintly defiant expression on her face. She was a tiny girl, maybe an inch over five feet. She didn't look as if she weighed a hundred pounds.

Sadie spotted Kate and came toward their table, but as she drew nearer she saw Hawk. Her steps slowed, and for a moment it looked as though she might take off. He braced himself to give chase, but she came forward reluctantly.

She looked as tough as he remembered, her long hair a shade of unnatural blond, her eyes lined and the mascara too thick, her lips a vampire red. She was wearing a black leather jacket and a red miniskirt. Today, though, he could see a certain weariness under her tough mask, and he felt inordinately pleased to see the girl. Alive.

"What?" she asked Kate, ignoring him.

"We just wanted to see if you were all right," Kate said gently. "Your family has filed a missing persons report."

Sadie sank onto the bench seat beside Kate. "Mickey didn't send you? He's the only one who knows where I am. I thought maybe something had happened to him."

"Is that the boy in the green truck?" Kate asked. It was evident the girl felt very strongly about Mickey.

She nodded. "My brother."

"He didn't tell us where you were."

"Then how—" Her eyes fell on Hawk and stayed there. "I suppose I'm in trouble, aren't I?"

"For what?" he asked, making a conscious effort to not use his get-out-of-the-car-with-your-hands-up tone of voice.

She looked baffled. Absently she reached out and took the baby's hand. She smiled when that little hand tightened around her finger, and for a moment she looked like a very different girl. Her features softened and the hard wariness left her eyes. Hawk realized with surprise she would be quite lovely if she wore her makeup differently.

After a second she let go of the baby's hand. "I stole some money from my folks," she said, jutting her chin out at him. "Just to get here. I'm going to pay them back as soon as I get ahead. I work here. The bartender's my second cousin but he doesn't have much use for my parents."

Underneath the jutting chin and the fast talk, he saw her fear. She thought he was going to arrest her and drag her out of here in cuffs.

Sure. He did all his police work with a baby. Not to mention the Lilac Lady.

"I don't know anything about any money," Hawk said carefully, aware he did not want to make her any more afraid than she already was. "Your mother filed a missing persons report. I wanted to know where you were. I wanted to know you were all right."

Her chin dropped and she gave him an astonished look. "Really? *You* wanted to know I was okay?"

"Yeah," he said gruffly. "Really."

"How come?" Her eyes never moved from his, but she nervously pulled a piece of gum from a beat-up little red vinyl bag and popped it in her mouth.

He could have said it was his job, but he knew she needed something more than that. He was probably the last person on earth who could give her anything she needed, but he could feel Kate's eyes on him, willing him to say the right thing, begging him.

"Uh," he said, "you seem like a bright girl, Sadie, and spunky. I think you have something to give this old world, and I didn't want something to happen to you before you had your chance."

Her jaw stopped working. She regarded him long and hard. "Yeah, well," she said uncomfortably and ducked her head.

He looked helplessly at Kate. He'd tried. Kate was beaming at him.

"Would you not tell them where I am? My folks?"

He hesitated, but then he saw the desperation in her eyes and suddenly he felt as though he knew a whole lot about her and what she was running so hard from. He hoped she'd make it.

"I won't tell them where you are," he promised. "I'll let them know you're safe and happy."

"Well, safe," she said dryly, and then added softly, "Thanks."

He had a feeling that word came very hard to this hard girl in front of him, and that maybe the fact she could say it already meant she was on her way to a different kind of life.

"Do you know Samantha Height?" he asked her.

"Sure," she said, popping her gum.

"Do you know where she is?"

"You mean she's not home at the Posh Palace?" There was a certain bitter envy in the way she said that.

"No, her parents reported her missing about the same time yours reported you."

"Well, I'll be damned," Sadie said, something like a smile playing around the edges of her too-red lips.

"Do you know where she is?"

"No. But I know where I hope she is."

"And where is that?"

"With my brother."

"Mickey," he said slowly. The green truck. The connection. "Why?"

"She probably isn't. They had a thing. Last year. Mickey and Sam. Her parents, the good Dr. and Mrs. Hoity-Toity of Sleepy Grove, were hysterical about it when they found out. Can you imagine? A McGee and a Height?" She rolled her eyes.

"Anyway, the way I heard it, they threatened to send her to a convent or Switzerland or something. I thought she was a real wimp for knuckling under to them, myself. Mickey was pretty torn up about it."

He remembered feeling the Heights had kept something from him. The most important something, as it turned out. They were respected people, but he felt no respect for them. They had let their pride keep them from their best chance of finding their daughter. Never once had Mickey Mc-Gee's name been mentioned to him.

He exchanged a glance with Kate. He could see in her eyes that she was thinking the same thing as he was.

Great. He was on the same wavelength as the town kook. But even as he thought it, he knew he'd stopped thinking of her as a kook a long time ago. He forced himself back to the matter at hand.

"How torn up was Mickey?" he asked Sadie softly.

Sam had had a fling with the wrong boy from the wrong side of town. At the request of her parents, she had dropped him cold. How did that wrong boy feel about all that? Hurt? Angry? Hurt and angry enough to kidnap? Kill?

"If you're asking me if he would ever harm her, the answer is no," Sadie said shrewdly. "He wouldn't."

"Where's your brother living right now?" he asked, carefully, casually.

"Forget it," she said, not fooled.

"Come on, Sadie. If he didn't do anything, he has nothing to fear."

"She might be with him. Maybe she played it really cool, you know? Waited until school was over, waited until she was of legal age and then did what she wanted. You might force her to go back to her parents."

"Not me," he said. "She's an adult. She can do what she wants. I just want to know where she is."

"I can't help you," Sadie said stubbornly. "I don't know where he lives, anyway. He's kind of a bush boy, you know? He's always finding these little log cabins beside lakes to live in."

Water.

"No idea?" he pushed.

She shook her head. "None. Really."

He wasn't sure he believed her, but he recognized the stubborn set of her jaw. Still, he tried one last time.

"Where does he work?"

She shrugged. "Sometimes in auto body shops. Lately he's managed to sell a few paintings. He's really good."

"Oh, for heaven's sake," Kate said. "I have one of his paintings. Two children flying a kite."

Hawk felt a ripple of surprise. The rough-looking boy in the truck had painted *that?*

Sadie turned and gave her full attention to Kate. "He's pretty good, isn't he?"

"He's very good," Kate said warmly.

"You know, when Roly—" Sadie nodded at the man behind the bar "—called me and said the Lilac Lady was here, I kind of felt like I was having a visit from the tooth fairy or a fairy godmother."

Then she did something that Hawk wouldn't have believed her capable of. She blushed. "That's silly, huh?"

"I'm flattered you knew who I was," Kate said with grace and sincerity.

He tried to catch her eye. If Kate asked where the boy was Sadie would probably tell her. She seemed to be deliberately avoiding his gaze.

"Everybody knows who you are," Sadie was saying. "Is it true you kind of, like, have the sight?"

"Yes," Kate said uncomfortably.

"Is that how you found me?"

"It was certainly part of it."

"Wow," Sadie said, round-eyed. "Cool." Then her nose scrunched up. "Yuck. What's that smell?"

All three of them suddenly looked at the baby who chortled happily back at them.

"Don't worry about it," Kate said. "We have a newly versed expert right here."

Sadie flung her head around and stared at Hawk. "Not him?"

"None other," Kate told her.

Sadie started to laugh. "Next time I'm in Sleepy Grove I can't wait to tell the kids—"

Hawk leaned very close to her. "You have your secrets," he said grimly, "and I have mine." He scooped up the baby with great dignity, tucked her back under his arms, so that her little round fanny and legs were wagging at Kate and Sadie, and left the bar.

"What's with you and him?" Sadie asked baldly.

"Nothing," Kate stammered.

Sadie looked at her for a long and stripping moment and then smiled that same smile she'd given when she'd heard Samantha had disappeared. "Cool," she said.

"'The sight,'" Hawk mulled over, almost to himself, as they headed back toward Sleepy Grove.

Kate noticed the vehicle smelled overwhelmingly of after-shave.

"Is that what they call it?"

"I guess different people call it different things," Kate said, opening her window a few inches. English Leather?

"You really have it, don't you?"

"I didn't always, but yes, I seem to now."

"You didn't always? When did you get it? How?"

He was like a scientist now, probing and prodding. It worked, so now he had to know how it worked.

There was probably an explanation for the after-shave, too, but she couldn't think of any plausible one. He was not a secret drinker, she knew that.

"I had my first experience two years after the accident that took Carly and Jerry, just shortly after I moved to

Sleepy Grove." It had been a long time since she had said their names. They felt strange on her lips.

"I was visiting the lodge," she continued. "Mrs. Carruthers's daughter and granddaughter were there. The granddaughter was off playing somewhere. I stopped to say hello, and I noticed this teddy bear peeking out from underneath a bush. I thought it would get forgotten so I picked it up to give to them. It burned me."

"It burned you?"

"It was so hot I felt scorched by it. A second later these pictures started flashing through my brain. I could see a child crying, screaming, caught on a rock outcropping."

"No kidding," he breathed. "You know, I notice that embankment every time I drive by the old folks' home. It's really high and steep. It should be cordoned off."

"That's the one," Kate said. "To make a long story short, Mrs. Carruthers's granddaughter, owner of the teddy bear, had wandered off and fallen over the embankment. It was wonderful that she was all right, but the experience was quite awful. I had never had anything like that happen to me before.

"The police and fire department were called to help make the rescue and Mrs. Carruthers's daughter was telling anyone who would listen how we had found the child. I felt everyone looking at me as if I was some sort of witch. Two hundred years ago I suspect I'd have been burned at the stake despite the fact I had done a good deed."

She decided against telling him the most personal part of the drama. Through the whole thing, she had had the strangest sensation of Carly, her own daughter, being close to her, like a small guardian angel.

"Can you direct how it comes and goes?" Hawk asked.

"I seem to be able to. I mean I don't pull it out as a party game or anything like that." She had not been to a party in over six years, but she did not add that detail. "The only other times I've ever tried it have been at Chief Nordstrom's request."

"You don't like to use it, do you?" he asked shrewdly.

That was a more complicated question than he knew. Each time she had used it, she had felt Carly. But the strangeness of the experiences left her unsettled, and the results of her applying her "gift" were not always happy ones.

"If it helps people in need of aid," she answered him, "how can I not use it?"

"And has it?"

"I wouldn't want to give the impression Bill comes knocking on my door every second day. I think he's only asked for my help two or three times."

"Tell me about them."

"Once an old man with Alzheimer's had wandered away from home one afternoon. Bill brought me the man's watch after he'd been gone eight hours. We found him wandering around in the woods south of town."

"How?"

"I just kept seeing him. I could see a creek and trees, which wasn't very helpful because there are many areas around town that look like that. But I could also hear cattle. Bill and I drove around to all the dairy farms. One was on the edge of some woods, and the feeling I got was very strong there. Bill called out every available man on the strength of that feeling. They found him within an hour."

Hawk let out a low whistle. "That's impressive. What about the other?"

She shivered, suddenly feeling cold. The smell of the after-shave was so strong.

"It didn't end happily," she said abruptly.

"I'm sorry."

She could feel his eyes on her, gray and searching. She tried to will the blood back into her face.

"Kate, are you all right?"

"She was dead. I saw her."

He was silent for a long time. "I'm sorry you had to see that. Even people trained to deal with it don't handle it well. I don't."

He had seen real dead bodies. She didn't want to know how many or why, though she was a step closer to understanding the coolness she had seen in his eyes so often.

And even though he might think less of her, she could not let him harbor his current misconception about her.

"I didn't actually *see* her. Not like that. But it was bad enough."

"You mean—"

"I held her wedding ring and saw the body in an illegal dumping area."

Before she knew it, she was filling him in on all the gory details of the case. She had never talked about it. Was it the fact that he had probably seen and experienced much worse that made it so easy to tell him?

When she was done she felt good for a moment and then suddenly sick. "Could you stop for a minute? I just need a bit of fresh air."

He pulled over rapidly, and she went to unbuckle the baby, wondering if that smell was bothering Brittany as much as it was her.

It was when she leaned over to the baby that she realized the truth.

The smell was not coming from Hawk at all.

"You put after-shave on the baby," she said with disbelief, her queasiness vanishing.

A funny shade of brick red rose up the strong column of his throat. "Uh, I couldn't find her stuff. But I'd left a bottle of after-shave in the gym bag."

"Babies have very delicate skin!"

"So do men after they shave! Besides, I didn't put it on *her*, just on the outside of the diaper. Like a deodorant."

She took the baby and stood outside in the sunlight, her shoulders shaking with laughter, the dark memories washed from her mind. He had stopped the vehicle along a particularly pretty stretch of road. The ponderosa pine was tall and thick, the scent heavenly.

After a while she set the baby down on the seat and, leaning in the door, she changed her diaper. She put the dress on the right way and then stood again, not wanting to move for some reason, the sun feeling so good on her face, the baby so wonderful in her arms.

He came and stood beside her. She noticed he smelled of soap. No after-shave at all. He was a hair away from her, and she could feel the sun-warmed heat radiating from his skin.

"I'm sorry I never believed you at first."

She shot him a surprised look. He was looking deliberately away, as if the traffic pattern fascinated him endlessly.

"There's a time when I wouldn't have believed it myself, Hawk."

"You should have talked to someone about it before," he said softly.

How could she tell him there had been nobody to talk to, without sounding completely pathetic?

For a moment their eyes met, and she felt a quiver of pure anticipation. Her awareness suddenly seemed sensuously heightened. The sky seemed intensely blue behind him, the trees iridescent. The soap scent tickled her nostrils. His eyes were like a lake she had seen once, long ago, high in the alpine. Shades of gray, reflecting stone. His lips were firm and full, and she knew suddenly, giddily, that he felt the moment as intensely as she did. He was going to kiss her.

He leaned toward her.

Her breath stopped and her heart started.

Brittany crowed, strained upward within Kate's embrace and with a pudgy hand tried to grab her uncle's nose.

He dodged her deftly and laughed, but the shimmering sensuality of the moment was lost.

Kate was taken aback by how acutely she felt that loss.

"We should go," she stammered, as if she had a full social calendar waiting for her, instead of a few hours of weeding.

"We should," he agreed too readily, turning abruptly away from her. "I want to catch Bill before he leaves the office for the day."

Chapter Six

"Can you wait here for a minute with Brittany?" he asked, putting his vehicle in park in front of the Sleepy Grove police station. "I'm on days off but I'd just like to let Bill know we can close the file on Sadie."

"I suppose the guys would give you a pretty hard time if you went in there with a baby," she said.

He grinned. "The phrase *hard time* would take on a whole new meaning."

His teeth were incredibly white and straight. That dimple pressed deeply into the side of his cheek.

She ached, with a physical ache, for that kiss that had not happened at the side of the road, and she despised herself for wanting it.

"Of course I'll stay with Brittany." Her voice was deliberately cool, as if she was a professional nanny. She did not want to let him know the awful truth. She had the uneasy feeling she would have baby-sat a baby gorilla for him if he asked. In exchange for a few kisses from that incredible mouth.

She did not like what she was feeling at all. It felt like a feeling she should be fighting against with all her might.

She had been alone for many years—which had its downside. But one of the positives was the growing sense of personal power that she had been feeling.

She was not going to be sad enough and silly enough to throw that away because he had a nice smile.

Not, she reminded herself, that he had asked her to throw anything away.

She watched him sprint lightly up the stairs and go through the double glass doors into the old brick building.

A nice smile and a nice derriere.

"I don't like athletic men," she informed the baby defiantly. Though she wasn't quite sure what there was to dislike about all those muscles and the way his jeans hugged his firm rear end.

A policeman in uniform came out the door Hawk had just gone in. For some reason she noticed the gun, heavy and black, on his hip.

A reminder that these men were prepared to kill or be killed in defense of the citizens of Sleepy Grove.

Her dentist, she recalled, had shyly asked her for a date the last time she'd had a checkup. The next time he asked, she would say yes. There was nothing dangerous in dentistry. Dr. Phelps was exactly what she should be looking for in a man.

Which she hadn't been doing until *he* came along, she realized peevishly.

So this would be the end of it. "I should offer to help with you," she said, apologizing to Brittany, who was bent over double and grunting in her effort to get both her socks off her feet, "but I can't."

She looked again at where Hawk had disappeared through the door. "I just can't," she whispered.

"I found Sadie McGee," Hawk told Bill upon entering his office. Quickly he went over the details with him, including the parts about Mickey and Samantha.

"Mickey McGee and Samantha Height?" The chief whistled. "No, Dr. Height wouldn't like that one little bit. I always liked Mickey, though."

"He looked like a hood to me," Hawk said.

"Oh, sure. Lots of the kids look like that. Have you seen any of his paintings? Wilma really likes them."

Hawk sighed. Was this any way to conduct police work? "I don't suppose Wilma knows where he lives, does she?"

"I'll ask her," Bill said happily, oblivious to Hawk's faint undertone of sarcasm. "Speaking of Wilma, she's got a favor she wants me to ask of you. I suppose you've heard about this awful thing with Tim Ryan?"

Hawk nodded. The little boy had some sort of rare kidney ailment. At every cash register in town was a can collecting money to help pay for his medical treatments.

"Wilma's organizing an auction with proceeds going toward paying his medical expenses. Can she count on your help?"

It wasn't until after he'd said "of course" that Hawk noticed a funny little twinkle in the chief's eye.

"Great. That makes a dozen of you."

"A dozen of us what?" Hawk asked suspiciously.

"Bachelors."

"Bachelors?" Hawk echoed. "I don't understand."

"It's a bachelor auction."

Hawk hoped he was misunderstanding something.

But he wasn't. The chief filled him in cheerfully on how it worked. "A nice dinner, some nice prizes like perfume and rings and then an auction of all the most eligible men in North Idaho. Women will probably come from miles around.''

"No," Hawk said.

"Oh, it's just for a date. Slavery's been abolished, you know, though Wilma'd probably raise more money if they got to keep you for a week." He chuckled, somehow missing the death rays Hawk was sending out of his eyes. ''You just take them on one date. Out for dinner or something.''

His smile faltered, and Hawk figured Bill was finally seeing the killer his sister said lurked in Hawk's eyes. "The department will pay for the dinner," he said hastily.

"This," Hawk bit out every word carefully, "is the most idiotic idea I have ever heard."

The chief's face got quite red. "It was Wilma's idea," he said softly.

"Well, I can't do it," Hawk said. "I can't go up in front of a bunch of women and get auctioned off like a side of prize beef. I can't. I won't."

"You know, Hawk," the chief said slowly, "you're a good cop. Maybe even the best I've seen. But sometimes I can't figure what kind of man you are. You got no sense of humor. What's wrong with having a little laugh at yourself?"

"What's wrong with helping by setting up a few tables?" he shot back.

"You won't put your own ego on hold to help a little boy in trouble?"

"I'll give him half my next paycheck," Hawk said darkly. Bill was getting a very stubborn look on his face.

"You'll be in the damned auction. It'll be good for you. This is the type of thing small towns are about. If caring about each other seems corny to you, maybe you just don't belong here. Maybe it's time we found that out."

"Are you saying you'll fire me if I don't go in the auction?" Hawk demanded.

Bill suddenly looked tired. "Nope, son, I'm not saying that. I'm asking you to stretch, I'm asking you to peek over that wall you got around yourself, I'm asking you to be a part of the town, I'm asking you to learn to laugh at yourself. And most of all I'm asking you not to hurt my wife's feelings."

Nothing else had moved him, so he was very surprised that he didn't want to hurt Wilma's feelings. "Aw, hell, Bill."

Five months ago he wouldn't have given a hoot for a little old lady's feelings.

It occurred to him he could lie. He could walk Bill over to the window and point at Kate, waiting in the vehicle, and say, "My girlfriend wouldn't be too thrilled."

He'd be killing two birds with one stone. He wouldn't have to be in the auction, and Wilma would probably stop inviting him for dinners that included the single women of Sleepy Grove.

But he remembered the look on Kate's face when he had briefly considered telling a small lie to that bartender today.

Four months ago he wouldn't have given a little white lie told to preserve his own dignity one thought.

Something was changing in him. And he wasn't sure he liked it one little bit.

Bill smiled at him. "I thought you'd see it my way. Wilma will be in touch...with the details about what to wear and such."

"Uniform?" Hawk asked tersely.

"Nah. I think Wilma said something about shorts."

"Shorts," Hawk repeated with disbelief. "Shorts."

* * *

Kate could tell something was wrong as soon as he came back out of the station. He got in the truck and shut the door with a small click that was far more telling than a slam.

He said nothing to her. He stared straight ahead and started the engine with a snap of his wrist. The tires squealed ever so slightly as he pulled swiftly out of the parking spot.

"Is something wrong?"

He still didn't look at her. "No."

"Oh."

He drove her home, his mouth in a tense line. He reached over the baby and her lap and opened the door.

She felt stunned. He might as well have said, "Get out." She started to do just that, feeling furious, even though she had decided already to have nothing more to do with him.

She'd spent the whole day with him. They'd accomplished their goal. Now she'd outlived her usefulness and was being tossed out of his vehicle without so much as a thank-you.

Hey, I'm the same woman you nearly kissed not half an hour ago.

See, she told herself, Providence had intervened. What if she *had* kissed him and he still acted like this?

If it wasn't for that baby, she might have told him where to go in very unladylike terms.

She tried to think if she'd ever done that to anyone in her entire life. She realized she hadn't. Too bad about the baby, because she realized she wanted very badly to be unladylike.

"Kate?"

Something in his voice stopped her just before she slammed the door. Hard. Something in his voice drew her back to him, even though she wanted to march up her walk with her nose in the air and close her front door firmly behind her.

"Have you heard of this thing for Tim Ryan?"

It was not what she was expecting. She looked at him through the window of the truck. "The dinner fundraiser?" she asked, puzzled.

He nodded bleakly. "And an auction."

"I hadn't heard about the auction."

"Bachelors," he said tersely.

"Bachelors?" she echoed, not sure what he was getting at.

"Kate, they're auctioning bachelors."

She didn't understand why he was telling her this or why he seemed so tormented. She did know her anger was gone as though it had never existed.

Suddenly her heart did a funny little leap and spin. Was he saying he didn't want her to go? Because there would be bachelors there? Did he really think she was the type of woman who would be interested in that kind of thing?

When she obviously didn't get it, he sighed a big sigh.

"Kate, I'm a bachelor."

"Oh, no," she said, her eyes growing round as the full implication of what he was saying hit her. "Oh, Hawk."

It was so ludicrous she had bite the side of her cheek, hard, to keep from laughing.

It frightened her that her emotions, usually so controlled, became so unfrozen around him, bubbling uncomfortably close to the surface.

"It was the chief's wife's idea," he said by way of explanation. His dignity was so obviously genuinely wounded. "You have to help me."

"I don't see how—"

"I'll give you some money. I'll pay for the dinner. But you have to be the one who buys me."

"Hawk, I don't go to things like that." Besides, she was resolved to take up with a dentist.

"Neither do I!"

He was trapped in a situation totally at odds with his character. And he was asking her to help him.

Perhaps there were some who would be strong enough to walk away from this odd offering of his trust, but she discovered she was not one of them.

"All right," she said resignedly. She started to walk away from the truck. Against her own will and better judgment she turned back to him. "If you need any help with Brittany let me know."

"Thanks," he said. "You're a real pal."

She watched him drive away. She was not sure what she wanted to be to Hawk Adams.

She would have liked to say "nothing" but she knew that not to be true. And she knew she did not want to be his "pal" either.

She knew something else. Despite her best efforts she seemed to be getting more and more tangled up in his life.

And she had laughed today in a way she hadn't laughed since her own little baby had tugged at her hair and her heart.

"What's happening to me?" she pondered.

Kate wondered, of course, how he was doing with the baby, but she refused to go see. She assumed he must be at his sister's house, and the temptation to just drive by and see if they were out for a walk or out in the yard was great. She resisted with all her might. Part of her wished for the phone to ring . . . for his voice, strangled with panic, to be at the other end of the line. But that didn't happen, and she stoically told herself it was for the best.

She went for groceries, trying to tell herself it was just the oddest of coincidences that she needed groceries again. The store was quite near his sister's.

She was stopped at the four-way intersection just west of the grocery store, when she saw it. The green truck, headed in the other direction.

Fully intending to follow it, she turned around, but by the time she was pointed in the right direction, the truck was nowhere to be seen.

She drove to Hawk's sister's house.

He came to the door after the second time she rang the bell. He opened the door and looked at her. He smiled, but his whole body seemed to be blocking the door.

He didn't want her in that house.

She was glad she had an excuse to be there. She would have felt foolish if she'd been making a social call, and he'd made it so apparent how unwelcome she was.

"I saw the truck," she told him with polite coolness, "the green truck that Sadie's brother drives."

His whole stature changed. "What? Where? When?"

"Going east on Redding. I turned around to follow him—"

"You did what?" he bellowed, grasping her arm and shepherding her into the kitchen.

She saw immediately why she hadn't been invited in. The mess was everywhere. Baby's toys and clothes. There were a few food splotches on the floor. There was the distinct odor of a puppy, mingled with baby smells.

She realized he looked exhausted.

Brittany cooed out her greeting. She was sitting in the middle of the kitchen floor, busily emptying a laundry basket. She wore a pair of large men's underwear on her head and what looked to be a very fancy party dress. A puppy snoozed next to her.

"A puppy?" Kate asked incredulously. "A—"

But Hawk was on the phone. "Where again, Kate? East on Redding? Five minutes ago?"

At her affirmative, he went back to talking on the phone. He hung up. "They're all looking for him now."

"A puppy?" she said.

He looked at his niece and the puppy. "I thought it would be nice."

"Nice?" Kate repeated.

"I thought it would keep her busy. You know, long enough for me to grab a shower or a sandwich. Kate, how the hell do mothers do it?"

"Without the puppy," she said succinctly.

"He didn't help," Hawk said, but with a notable lack of regret. He went and scooped the puppy up and held him back admiringly. "Purebred shepherd."

"Is it for her, or a police dog?"

"I had one when I was a boy. His name was Rex."

"Oh. That certainly explains it."

"Every kid should have a dog."

"She's too young for a dog."

"This way they'll grow up together," he said stubbornly.

She could see there was going to be no talking sense to him. He was looking at the puppy with boyish affection.

"Are you going out?" she asked him. She had given him the message about the truck. Why not just leave? It was obvious she had caught him at a very bad time. But somehow she felt she would be remiss to leave him like this.

"Going out?"

"Brittany's dress looks…like a going-out dress." At least it looked as though it had been a going-out dress once. The lace, now soggy and covered with the remains of a teething biscuit, looked as if it may have been antique. The red velvet was crushed beyond repair. It was not a playing-on-the-floor-with-the-puppy dress, though she refrained from saying so for the time being.

"Does it?" he asked, squinting at his niece. Then he sank into the nearest chair. A toy squeaked underneath him, and he reached back, pulled it out and tossed it away without missing a beat. "Do you want something?"

"Oh, no," she stammered.

"I meant tea or coffee."

She smiled her relief that he wasn't baldly asking her why she was hanging around. She carefully moved three cookies and a rubber doggie bone from the chair across from him.

"Careful where you put the doggy bone," he said, "Brittany's quite taken with it."

She looked at Brittany, who, having successfully emptied the laundry basket, was now filling it back up. She remembered how much Carly had liked this very same activity.

"What did you mean you were going to follow him?" he asked abruptly, his brows drawn down darkly.

"You wanted to know where he lived. I just thought—"

"If you ever even think it again, I'll—"

"You'll what?" she challenged him. She was a grown woman. She had been living independently long enough that she didn't need this big, arrogant man thinking he was going to tell her what to do!

He took a deep breath, as if he was trying for patience. "There's no need to get in a huff. It makes your freckles stand out. I'm just trying to tell you it wasn't a safe thing to do."

"I didn't do it," she reminded him. *Her freckles stand out?*

"Okay. It wasn't a safe thing to *think* about doing."

"That boy would not hurt anyone. You've seen the picture he painted—"

His attempt at patience was over. He was up out of his chair and leaning over her menacingly.

"We don't know yet if he's dangerous or not, and until we do, if you see that truck, you phone me or the police station, you don't follow it. Do I make myself perfectly clear? Lots of nuts paint pictures and write poems and stuff like that."

He was very intimidating this close. And gorgeous. And she'd die before she let him know she thought either.

She looked at him with flashing eyes, refusing to answer his question.

He glared back at her.

She should get up and leave, but somehow she wanted to now even less than before. "I'll have that tea now," she said snootily.

He backed away from her and began slamming through his sister's cupboards. Brittany's attention was diverted from the laundry basket, and she crawled over to one of the cupboards he'd left open and began to methodically and loudly empty the contents out of it.

Hawk ignored her. The puppy peed on the floor and he ignored that, too.

"How are things with your sister?" Kate asked cautiously, trying to cross the dangerous ground between them. A few more days and this house might well be beyond repair.

"She called. Her father-in-law is improving a lot. Jack's going to stay down one more day, but she's flying home tonight." He could not keep the relief out of his voice.

Kate couldn't help but glance around the kitchen. What a thing to be coming home to.

"I'm going to clean it up," he said defensively.

"Hawk, why didn't you just ask for help?" she asked quietly.

"Because," he snapped, "real men don't ask for help. Where the hell is the kettle?"

She got up and pulled it gingerly from behind a blender that looked as if it contained a rare form of mold. She held it out to him, and he grabbed it from her and went and filled it.

She plucked a paper towel from the holder and went over to the doggy spot.

"Don't touch that," he said tersely. "I can manage."

"It looks like it," she said back.

"You wouldn't invite me over to your house and then ask me to do housework."

"You didn't invite me," she reminded him, swabbing up the mess. When she was finished she opened the door under the sink.

"How did you get that door open?" he asked. "Mary's got some kind of sneaky lock on it."

"It's childproofed," Kate said approvingly. She showed him how to work the catch. "You don't want a baby getting into this stuff." She held up a bottle of yellow, lemon-scented cleaner.

"No, I guess not," he said, watching her douse another paper towel with the cleaner and go over the puppy spot. "Geez," he groaned.

"The baby is crawling around on this floor." She was aware he thought she was Miss Prim and Proper. Why did she care what he thought?

"Sit down and have this tea," he ordered when she began to pick things up to put in the laundry basket. "I said I'd look after it, and I will."

She looked at him and the mess. It didn't seem possible he could. But the look on his face said he would.

She sipped the tea. "So," she said casually, "what else don't real men do?"

"They hardly ever drink tea, and they only change diapers in an emergency and only then if any witnesses are sworn to secrecy."

"Sadie's going to tell if she has a chance," Kate warned him with a smile, the tension dissipating between them, like a summer storm breaking up.

"I know," he said tragically. The puppy came over and sat at his feet, looking at him with naked adoration. He picked it up with ease he had yet to demonstrate with the baby.

"What should we call him? I kind of like Tex."

"Maybe you should make sure your sister is going to keep him before you give him a name."

"Of course she's going to keep him," he said with surprise. "Why wouldn't she? My sister loves dogs, unlike you."

Were men born knowing nothing? If his sister loved dogs that much she would undoubtedly have one. Instead of pointing that out to him, she said, "What makes you think I don't like dogs?"

"Pepper. Right up his nose. Mrs. Meable."

"Measly," she said, correcting him, astonished by his memory.

He had a fine memory. Smart. Intelligent. Keenly intelligent. He probably saw too much. Far too much. Young widow giving in to loneliness.

"I'll go now," she said stiffly.

"Don't go," he said softly with a faint promise in his voice.

"Really, I—"

"I'm nearly out of my mind. You're the first grown-up I've talked to in more than twenty-four hours. Just stay."

"I really—"

"Brittany's going to bed soon."

Sure enough, his niece was stretching out on top of the emptied laundry, thumb finding its way to her mouth, eyes moving to half-mast.

"We really should clean up the house for your sister."

He groaned. His eyes were intense on her face. "Maybe we should do something else."

"Like what?" she heard herself asking, her voice a panicked squeak.

"Blue Jays are playing."

She was so surprised she didn't know whether to laugh or cry. "I don't think I like baseball."

"What do you mean you don't think?"

"Well, I don't exactly know."

He was looking at her narrowly.

Suddenly he was out of the chair. Stepping lithely over his now-snoring niece, he came and took her hand.

"I'm about to teach you everything you need to know about baseball."

She could feel the warmth of his hand, feel his eyes looking into hers.

Run a little voice inside her head yelled.

But she didn't. She said, "You're on," and followed him back over the sleeping baby, past the puppy who was shredding a variegated fig tree and into the living room.

There, among the debris of a puppy, a baby and a bachelor, they watched baseball, laughed and ate scorched popcorn.

When she finally caught on enough to cheer when one of his beloved Blue Jays hit a homer in the top of the eighth, he rewarded her by giving her the Blue Jays cap he had donned the moment the game began.

She stuck it on her head, and he looked at her and frowned.

"Not like that. It's not lucky like that."

He took the cap and turned it, so the bill faced backward.

"Better? But what does my hair look like?"

He contemplated her for a moment. "Worse," he decided.

She started to pull the cap off, but his strong hand stayed hers.

"You look cute. I'll fix your hair." Clumsily, he moved a few wisps here and there, then grinned at her, his fingers lingering on the edges of her face.

But she was not grinning. Her heart was suddenly hammering in her throat. It had been a long time since anyone had called her cute. It had been a very long time since strong fingers had touched her hair and trailed over her face.

"Home run!" the announcer screeched.

"You are lucky!" he said, his attention completely diverted. "Keep the cap."

And then casually, barely tearing his eyes away from the television set, as if they had known each other for a hundred years, and would know each other for a hundred more, he kissed her on the tip of her nose and wrapped his arm around her shoulder.

It did not feel casual to her. It felt like her heart was going to explode inside her chest. She felt warm and lovely and alive. She could not remember when she had had such a good time, when she had felt so connected to another human being.

She felt scared to death and pathetic. It was such a small thing, to sit here and watch a baseball game with a man.

She'd gotten out of touch with reality, that's what had happened. She couldn't do normal everyday things that normal everyday people did anymore, without them feeling big and earth-shattering somehow.

"I have to go," she said, leaping up from under the weight of his arm.

"No way. It's the bottom of the ninth."

"I just remembered something. An appointment. Dr. Phelps. The dentist."

She could see the confusion on his face and understood it perfectly. She was not being rational. In fact, she had not been rational since the moment she'd first met him.

It had to change. It had to change now.

She went back through the kitchen and over the baby. The puppy attached himself to the leg of her pants as she hurriedly put her shoes on.

She was aware of Hawk watching her, big muscular arms folded over his big, muscular chest.

He was so male. She absolutely yearned for him.

She could have made a safe getaway, if it hadn't been for the puppy's sharp little teeth being so hard to disengage from the hem of her jeans.

"See you soon," Hawk said. He leaned close.

His mouth dropped over hers. His mouth looked so hard and firm.

It felt soft and wonderful and tasted like raindrops.

She stood, stunned, the baseball cap still on backward and her mouth hanging open. She came to her senses, took one last look into the gray mystery of his eyes and dashed out the door.

He watched her leave, aware of a funny singing in his heart. When she had pulled away, and there was really absolutely no reason to stand there any longer looking at the place where she had been, he turned and regarded the mess. He smiled to himself, opened the phone book, and dialed a number. "Hello, is this Mrs. Clean Cleaning Service? I have a bit of an emergency on my hands...."

Kate didn't know why she had woken. The light in her room was still the soft pastel of earliest dawn. She'd been having a dream that she regretted leaving. It hovered briefly around the edges of her mind. It had something to do with strong arms and a hard chest, the Blue Jays and him.

She was aware suddenly of a pounding on her door. She glanced at her clock and then wrapped herself in her favorite old housecoat, faded blue and flocking, and went to the door.

She opened it carefully a notch. Hawk stood there, a big man who looked bigger, more intimidating in his uniform. The puppy squirming under his arm was all that softened the image.

At least, she told herself, she didn't have a baseball cap on. Backward.

"It's six in the morning," she told him, opening the door all the way.

"I know. I have to be at work in half an hour. Did you look through your peephole before you answered the door?"

"I don't even have a peephole, even if I had been awake enough to look through it," she informed him grouchily.

He looked at her door. "I'll put one in for you. It only takes a minute." He squinted at her door. "And a dead bolt. I can't believe you don't have a dead bolt."

"Well, thank you for waking me up at six in the morning to give me a lecture on my security measures," she said. "I suppose you'd like coffee, too?"

He smiled, and the remoteness left his face and his eyes. He was the Hawk who had coached her through her first ball game yesterday and put the cap on backward and sat with her on the couch with his arm around her shoulder as if it was the most natural thing in the whole world.

And kissed her.

"I don't have time for coffee. I came to ask a favor."

"Brittany?" she asked. "Where—"

"No, she's fine. Mary got home right on schedule."

"Oh. I'm glad."

"She doesn't want the dog. She wasn't even nice about the way she told me," he said glumly. "After I looked after Brittany and had her house cleaned—"

"You cleaned the house?"

"A miracle named Mrs. Clean cleaned the house. The point is, Mary might have been nicer about the way she told me."

Kate realized he must have his uniform cleaned and pressed professionally. It made her see something human beyond the hard image, just as the puppy had.

"Puppies can be a little difficult to manage if your schedule is already overloaded," she told him sympathetically.

"No pets in my apartment, either. I kept him last night, but the building manager was waiting for me this morning."

"That's too bad." For some reason, her eyes kept drifting to his lips. How on earth could they have tasted like raindrops?

"So, I kind of need a place to keep him. You know. Just for a day or two."

"Here?" she squeaked.

"He won't be any trouble. You can keep him outside. Your backyard is fenced. I'll come feed him. And clean up after him."

She would have said no. She should have said no. She couldn't say no. He'd be there twice a day looking after his dog.

"All right," she said. "You can put him in the backyard."

"Really?" His whole face brightened up boyishly. A funny feeling tickled at her and then was gone. "Thanks a lot, Kate. You're a real pal."

He was down the walk and around the side of the house in moments, looking strong and full of energy, the bright spring sunshine playing off the darkness of his hair.

She went to her kitchen window and watched him play with the puppy for a few minutes before he left for work. It was a lovely sight, and she had to wonder what she had let herself in for.

Nothing, she told herself. She was just his "pal." That's the way it needed to be.

There had been nothing passionate about his kisses yesterday. Nothing at all.

Friends. As soon as it started becoming anything else, she would nip it in the bud. Because she had to.

Because she knew only too well what a broken heart felt like.

She sighed as she watched him. He was gorgeous.

And suddenly he was coming back toward her, running, taking the steps up to the kitchen door two at a time.

"Kate?" he called, pulling open the screen and squinting against the sudden change in light.

"What?" she asked, almost irritably.

"Just this." He took one long step across her kitchen, scooped her and her ratty housecoat close to him and kissed her hard, right on the lips.

"Thanks again," he called as he ran back out the door.

"And thank you," she whispered, touching her lips where they still tingled.

She had been right after all. His lips tasted like raindrops.

Chapter Seven

"Hawk, I think I found a home for the puppy."

Kate's words sent a ripple of shock through him. The puppy, he called him Texas, had been at Kate's for a week.

He had thought everything was working out fine. Well, pretty much fine. He cleaned up after it and came twice a day to feed it.

He enjoyed those two times a day more than he cared to admit. He'd started coming a little earlier each morning, supposedly to play with the puppy. But she always got up and made a pot of coffee and brought it outside to him, steaming and rich, not like the syrupy tar he would have later at the station.

Early in the morning she usually dressed in snug-fitting jeans and a hooded pullover against the morning chill. Her hair had a certain untamable quality about it that was especially evident in the morning. With her face freshly scrubbed and free of makeup, she looked wholesome, the all-American girl become a woman.

At night, after work, he'd stop by again. By then she'd be in shorts, or a casual skirt, her shapely legs bare, her hair under control, a faint dusting of makeup trying to hide her freckles.

And he thought she'd enjoyed those daily visits, too. Two nights ago she'd invited him to stay for dinner. She'd stood at the stove whipping up fettucine Alfredo as if there was absolutely nothing to it. He'd sat at the table and she'd talked to him over her shoulder, telling him about the puppy's first encounter with the mailman.

"At first he was so ferocious!" Kate had turned and bared her teeth at him and growled so convincingly that he'd burst out laughing. "He tried to hold his ground when Dave just kept coming, but at the last moment he turned and ran, yelping, and hid under the lilacs."

Her voice had flowed over him, warm and laughter-filled, and he hadn't known when he'd felt so at home in all his life. There were fresh flowers on her table, and slowly the kitchen had started to fill with the aroma of garlic and spices.

"How was your day?" She'd taken a tiny taste of the sauce right off the spoon, and he hadn't been able to help but notice her lips.

The lips that were off-limits. She'd acted like a frightened schoolgirl that night he'd kissed her while they were watching ball, and she'd frozen in his arms the morning he'd dropped the puppy off.

He'd vowed to himself to hold off a bit.

But it was tougher than he ever could have imagined it would be.

He'd succeeded that night, though. He'd dragged his eyes away from her lips on the spoon and told her about giving eighty-two-year-old Maybelle Swift a speeding ticket.

"Hawk!"

"She was going ninety miles an hour through a playground zone!"

"Ninety?"

"I swear. And when I pulled her over she called me a young whippersnapper. She got out of her car and started hitting me with her umbrella."

"She did not!"

"She did. I told her to knock it off or I was going to book her for assault."

"You're making this all up."

"No, I'm not. Look at the bruise." He'd opened his shirt a button or two, and pulled it down off his shoulder.

She'd come and regarded his injury solemnly, while he prayed she'd think to kiss it better.

Instead she'd turned back to her sauce.

"Then she started telling me she'd known my daddy back when he was in wet diapers, and that he'd been the town's worst hooligan, and it didn't say a lot for the law that Martin Manhurst's son was allowed to become a cop. I told her I wasn't Miles Manhurst, who, by the way, has red hair and is six inches shorter than me.

"She squinted real hard at me, snorted and said she'd forgotten her glasses at home." He'd been so pleased to see Kate chortling happily as she stirred the sauce.

"Blind as a bat," he'd continued, "and she's driving her car a hundred miles an hour through a playground zone."

"I thought it was ninety," Kate had reminded him with a fiendish grin.

"Just checking to see if you were listening. Anyway, I wrestled her car keys away from her, which was harder than you might imagine, put her in the back seat of the cruiser and drove her home. She hit me with her damned umbrella the whole way! Do you want to see the rest of the bruises?"

He'd actually made her blush. Or maybe not. Maybe it was the heat coming out of that big pot of boiling pasta.

"Supper's ready," she'd said, ignoring his invitation. But he'd been pretty sure Kate Shea liked what was underneath his shirt.

She'd set a big plate of noodles and sauce in front of him, put a crisp salad on the table and a wicker basket full of buns still steaming from the oven.

A man could sell his soul for food like that. Or sign up for cooking class.

He'd watched her for a moment, neatly rolling her fettucine against her spoon, and suddenly felt big and awkward and as if he didn't know how to eat.

She'd glanced up at him and, with a twinkle in her eye, speared a noodle with her fork and sucked it up, dispelling his discomfort in a second—though unfortunately making him very aware of her damned lips again.

He'd done it, then, too, and she'd laughed, that wonderful, rich, straight-from-the-gut laugh of hers.

There'd been a smile in her eyes that was downright deadly.

A man could sell his soul for laughter like hers, too, and there was no class that was going to take away that feeling.

Which was probably why things had gotten out of hand last night.

Last night something had gone wrong. Or right depending how he looked at it. Things were moving along fairly platonically. There was a distance in her, and the once or twice he'd tried to cross it she'd bolted like a deer in front of hunters.

If he went too fast he was going to spook her, and that would be the end of it.

The end of coffee in the morning.

The end of fettucine Alfredo.

The end of those funny moments of shared laughter that made his insides feel better than they'd felt in about a hundred years.

The situation he was in right now was just about perfect for a confirmed bachelor like him. He had the pleasure of her company without the hassle of having to phone her and check in every ten seconds or so. He was getting the odd home-cooked meal without any of the usual strings attached.

It was a good thing, and he'd been tiptoeing around it like a Boy Scout walking his first old lady across the street.

But the truth of it was, Kate Shea was not bringing out the Boy Scout in him. And she was about as far from a little old lady as you could come. She looked a little too good in a pair of jeans and downright dangerous in a pair of shorts.

The strengthening spring sun was bringing out highlights in her hair and her cheeks that made him want to touch both—her hair with his hands, her cheeks with his lips.

There was a sparkle in her eyes that made him want to make her laugh forever.

Forever. There was that terrifying word again.

She was a forever kind of woman.

And she'd said those words to a man she'd buried. Her heart was pretty much on ice, he guessed, which brought him full circle. She should have been a safe bet for a born-again bachelor just like him.

And for a week he'd played Boy Scout, minding his manners, cleaning up the dog doo, acting as if she was his long-lost sister.

But yesterday he'd talked her into wrestling the dog with him, and somehow the dog had disappeared under the hedge and they'd ended up wrestling each other, at first laughing until they nearly choked as they rolled around on the green velvet of her lawn.

She'd been on top of him trying to keep him pinned. At first it had been just a game, but at some point it had begun to pierce him like a sharp knife—the way her soft muscles felt underneath that wide skirt, the softness of her skin when she touched him, the fullness of her breasts, the way her hair flew around her face in scattered curls, the way her lips shone like she'd just licked them.

Awareness of her had pierced him and ruined everything.

He couldn't ignore it, he couldn't pretend it wasn't there. Acting as if it was part of the game, he'd put his big mitt behind her neck and pulled her down toward him.

And proceeded to kiss the living daylights out of her.

A hunger that had matched his own had been there in her. Passion, pure and hard, and they'd barely had to scratch the surface to find it. Neither of them was even pretending it was a game anymore.

And then, without warning, just as he'd slid his hand under her shirt where it had pulled free from the skirt, just as he'd begun to explore the soft skin of her midriff, she'd yanked away from him, leapt up and stood a few feet away, breathing hard and looking at him like a frightened doe.

Looking at him accusingly, as if he'd been solely responsible for what had just happened.

He hadn't been invited for supper last night, no siree, and this morning when he'd arrived, there'd been no coffee brewing, and the curtains had been closed tight against him.

Now she was looking for a home for his puppy.

She had plenty of excuses. She hadn't been very happy about the roada-something that Tex had completely destroyed.

Or the pit in her garden that looked as if the puppy was digging through to China.

Come to think of it, the missing garden glove and the chewed-on rubber boot hadn't made her very happy, either.

And, he recalled, she refused to call Tex by his name. He was always "the puppy" to her, and occasionally "that rascal"—a dog, he realized, she was not going to get attached to.

She was right, of course. Tex needed a home. And not hers. And he knew it had everything to do with that stolen kiss, and not the roadadum-dums or whatever she called them.

"I've been thinking about buying a house," he heard himself saying.

He knew it was a ridiculous thing to say. That he was buying a house so he could have a dog. Maybe he should tell her he was going to sign up for cooking classes, too. That would probably really impress her. And, of course, he could show her his clumsy efforts to duplicate her own interior decorating.

But what was each of those things really saying? That he was longing for stability? That he was staying here in Sleepy Grove for good? A town that was going to auction him off to the highest bidder?

He amended hastily, "I mean not right away. The house." With his features frozen into what he could only hope was an easygoing mask, he said, "You're absolutely right. The dog needs a good home."

"Three boys came by here yesterday on their bicycles," she said quietly, her face as frozen as his. "They were quite taken with the dog."

He wanted to ask her if they'd come before or after that kiss, but there was really no point.

He felt a strange little squeeze around the region of his heart. Three boys. Could he ask for a better home for the dog? He might as well get it over with.

He scooped up the puppy. "Well, let's go," he said nonchalantly, as if he didn't care, as if he was *glad* she'd found a solution to the dog problem he hadn't even realized was a problem.

She was looking at him intently, as if she was trying to see the very thing he was trying to hide. She'd make a good poker player, trying to ferret out his feelings while playing her own so close to that enchanting chest. Well, he had a lot of experience at this game. He returned her look, coolly, even raised an inquiring eyebrow at her.

She sighed and put down her gardening gloves. "Your car or mine?"

He missed the woman who had laughed at him yesterday, her eyes as golden as sunshine, her laughter carefree as a young girl's, her hair tangled with leaves.

No leaves in that hair today. Every piece tortured into place. She was wearing some sort of touch-me-not blouse, with a high collar and a cameo closing off even a glimpse at the pale skin of her throat.

They went in his vehicle. The puppy wriggled in her lap and tried to lick her face.

She resisted, but he was inwardly rooting for the puppy. They arrived at the house, which was only a few blocks away, with her lipstick intact.

The signs of three rambunctious boys were everywhere. A tire swing hung limply from one tree, a baseball mitt underneath it. Three bikes had been thrown down on a lawn that was half-mowed. A few trampled perennials struggled in the flower bed. A basketball hoop and a hockey net stood in the driveway.

Tex was going to love it here.

They had no sooner gotten out of his truck when the boys, of various heights under four feet, blond and sturdy, tumbled out of the house.

Kate, still guarding her pristine lips by holding the puppy at arm's length, set Tex on the ground. Hawk allowed himself to feel a moment's adolescent pleasure that her blouse had a paw smudge on it.

Tex saw the boys. His tail went up and his ears pointed. Red alert. For a moment, regretfully, Hawk could see in the dog's bone structure the promise of strength and loyal companionship. Then Tex scampered toward the boys, his round fat body all aquiver, his tail waving wildly. In seconds, Tex had changed his allegiance completely, so engrossed was he in the rough-and-tumble play of the boys.

It reminded Hawk, painfully, of the "rough" he'd enjoyed yesterday. He'd missed the "tumble" part, however.

Was this ice queen beside him the same lady?

Kate went up the front steps and talked to the mother, who was looking at the ruckus with a weary expression. Hawk stayed where he was, watching the boys, the sunshine on their hair, the sound of their laughter mingling with the high-pitched puppy barks.

Kate came back down the walk. She stopped for just a moment, and Tex paused in his play long enough to accept one little scratch behind the ears. She stood and watched the puppy for a second as he turned and ran back to the boys, and for that second Hawk almost read regret into her features. But by the time she turned back to him, her expression was carefully blank again.

He realized he felt angry at her, not that he was going to let her see it.

They drove away in silence.

"It seemed like a very good home for him," she said.

He didn't reply. Ha. She was feeling guilty. He wanted to make her wallow in it, just the way he'd wallowed in guilt for committing the unpardonable sin of kissing her.

As if that wasn't what every other man and woman on the face of the earth were doing.

"You agree it's for the best, don't you?"

He could hear the worry in her voice.

"Oh, absolutely," he said insincerely.

"I didn't want to push you into something you weren't ready to do, but the boys came by on their bikes and mentioned they'd been looking for a dog. They just seemed so perfect for him."

Her voice trailed away lamely.

Put her out of her misery, Hawk instructed himself sternly. Instead he said pleasantly, "No roada-dentures in that yard."

She looked away. "I'm not equipped to look after a dog."

He knew he was being unfair. She was right. She was not equipped to look after a dog, and neither was he.

Both of them lived in self-imposed prisons of isolation. A puppy's insatiable need for affection might rattle the bars a bit.

So, of course, might hot, hungry kisses.

She was right. It was for the best. Get rid of the puppy.

So why did it feel like this big fist was closing on his chest?

Because it was more than the puppy. He wouldn't have an excuse to drop by her place two or three times a day anymore. No more wake-up coffee in the bright morning sunshine. No more fettucine Alfredo. No more spontaneous wrestling matches.

She was an easy woman to be with.

Until you tried to kiss her.

It was for the best that she didn't want his dog hanging around. It was for the best that she didn't want him hanging around, either.

He dropped her off at her house. He wondered if the next time he saw her would be at the house-of-horrors auction. He wondered if she'd still be willing to help him.

Somehow he couldn't bring himself to ask.

Kate watched him drive away from behind the shield of her living room curtains. She felt absolutely miserable.

Resolutely she marched into her bedroom and took off the pretty blouse and put on gardening clothes.

She would weed until her back ached and her hands blistered. She would work in her garden until thoughts of him went away and never came back.

The gardening season doesn't last that long, a little voice inside her head chided her.

She ignored it, bustled outside and went to work. She found a little ball, pierced with small teeth marks, in among the peonies. She set it beside her. There was a new hole, too, cleverly hidden in between the house foundation and a honeysuckle shrub.

She was glad the dog was gone, and as for *him*, well, who needed to be made a widow twice in one lifetime?

Not that umbrellas were exactly lethal assault weapons.

No, it wasn't just his job. It was the way he was making her *feel*. All tingly and excited, her cheeks hot as if she was blushing permanently.

Out of control.

Well, she was back in control now. No puppy and no man. Only it didn't feel nearly as good as she had thought it would, and every time she caught sight of that stupid ball out of the corner of her eye, she felt as though she was going to burst into tears.

Two days later the phone rang. She listened quietly to the excited singsong voice on the other end and then finally said, "Of course I'll come get him. No, it's perfectly understandable. Please don't worry about it."

Kate caught a glimpse of her own reflection on the way out the door. She was actually smiling. Her eyes had instantly lost that dull look that had been haunting them.

"For heaven's sake," she chided herself, "it's a puppy."

But she walked very fast to the house. Tex raced out of the yard and flung himself at her feet, yelping joyously.

He remembered her! He was glad to see her.

But not nearly, she suspected, as glad as she was to see him.

The tired-looking mother came out of the house and smiled at the commotion the dog was making at Kate's feet.

"He is not at home here," she said awkwardly. "He cries at night. He destroys things, no?"

Kate squatted down and picked him up. He licked her face and she let him.

"Oh, Tex," she scolded. "Are you a bad dog?"

She didn't think she'd ever said his name before.

The mother handed her a leash and gave a litany of the dog's sins, which were numerous in light of the length of his stay. Kate set Tex down and attached the lead to his collar. He immediately ran three times around her legs.

Laughing, she untangled him. "Come on, Tex, time to go home."

He seemed to understand that and lunged ahead with such strength he nearly pulled her arm out of her socket.

Hawk had just gotten off work and was debating yet another trip to the paint store, when he saw her being dragged down the sidewalk with Tex on the other end of the leash.

He couldn't believe his luck. A built-in excuse to stop and talk to her.

"Hey, lady," he said, pulling over to the curb, "nice dog." He could feel himself grinning like an idiot.

Her head flew up. "Oh," she said, and he could tell she was trying not to, but she smiled, too. She was wearing those nice faded denims that showed off her waist so well.

"Want a ride?"

She looked suddenly flustered, as though she wanted anything but. But the dog was being a menace, tugging her in every direction but the one she was going in.

She climbed into the car.

He put the dog in the back seat and ordered him to stay. He was pleasantly surprised when the dog listened.

"What happened?" he asked, not even trying to hide his pleasure.

"He destroyed a fifty-dollar baseball mitt and a goalie pad. He might have been forgiven that, but he tore the mother's brassiere off the laundry line and showed it to most of the neighborhood. He dug a pit large enough to find dinosaur bones in and then finished his short stay by eating most of the underlay off the living room carpet and then throwing up."

Hawk turned and gave the dog an approving look. Tex, exhausted, was fast asleep.

He shot Kate a look. If she was displeased about being pressed into the dog-sitting business once again, she didn't show it.

"I'll put an ad in the paper," he said, testing the waters.

"Or you could buy that house," she said softly.

He felt himself stiffen. What on earth was she suggesting? That they take that kiss somewhere he never intended for it to go? That he buy a little house and they set up housekeeping?

He shot her another look. She looked more herself today, her curls faintly untamed, her sunburn showing, now that her nose was unpowdered, her jeans old enough to fit just right over the perfect curve of her behind.

For a moment he was tempted to drive right to the real estate office.

But he was saved from himself when out of the corner of his eye, he saw it. The truck. The green truck.

With squealing tires he pulled a U-turn behind it. He noted her whitened knuckles on the dashboard.

He debated what to do next. He was in his own vehicle, with no radio. Though he was still in uniform, instinct told him he wouldn't get anywhere by pulling the boy over. He wondered if he had aroused suspicion by pulling the U-turn in the middle of the street.

Following behind, he noticed with satisfaction the boy was not watching his mirrors at all. All the windows in Hawk's vehicle were down, and he could hear McGee's music, very raunchy and turned up so loud he hadn't even heard the squealing tires.

"I'm going to follow him," he decided out loud. He cast Kate a quick glance. "Do you have a casserole burning in the oven or anything?"

He was rather pleased with the question. It might make her think he thought of her in the frumpy housewife category, rather than the beguiling lips category.

"No," she snapped.

"Good. Maybe you'll pick up some vibes or something." That was just to let her know he hadn't invited her for the pleasure of her company, just to let her know he'd completely washed that last kiss from his mind. *Completely.*

He grinned at her, liking all over again the way her eyes flashed when she was indignant.

They followed the green truck all the way past the town limits, Hawk falling way back when they finally turned off the highway onto an unpaved gravel road. The boy still seemed unaware he was being followed.

The road appeared to have no other traffic on it, and Hawk dropped way back, so that they occasionally just caught a glimpse of the truck going around a turn or cresting a hill.

The road came out of deep woods and began to wind beside the side of a lake. In a short time they began to see the occasional cottage beside the lake.

And then they saw the green truck parked under a giant cedar. A path led from the cedar to a very old cabin constructed of logs, long since weathered gray.

Hawk drove slowly by. Mickey McGee must have already gone into the cabin.

He went up the road beyond the cabin and then turned around and came back down slowly, mulling over his options thoughtfully.

"Hawk, stop."

He braked sharply, looked at her and then followed her gaze. From this angle he could see the lake and the dock in front of McGee's cabin.

And at the end of that dock, her feet swinging in the water, and her bright blond hair shining in the sun, sat a girl he was almost certain was Samantha Height.

"Sam!"

Hawk's head swiveled, and he saw Mickey McGee coming out of the cabin and across the expanse of lawn, waving a big brown square that looked like an envelope.

"Sam," Mickey called again, his voice young and strong and full of confidence.

The girl turned, and the look of light on her face nearly hurt Hawk's eyes, hardened soul that he was.

He watched her clamber to her feet and move toward the boy, her every move a dance created by exuberance.

The boy met her and gathered her in his arms, lifting her so her feet came off the ground and swung around him.

Her laughter and then his echoed with crystal clarity over the lake and back to the truck.

Hawk shot Kate a look.

The absolute magic of it was not lost on her. The love between that young couple shimmered in the air around them, a tangible thing.

Kate's face was soft with empathy. If he was not mistaken, an unshed tear or two sparkled behind her eyes.

He turned his attention back to the young couple. "It's like a painting, isn't it?" he said slowly.

She could only nod.

They watched the young couple for a few minutes more, until they linked hands and went toward the cabin, their heads dropped together in serious discussion.

When they went in the door and shut it behind them, he could feel Kate sigh beside him.

A romantic, he thought uneasily. Her husband had probably been good at flowers and poetry and gifts of chocolates and lingerie.

No wonder a kiss from a big lunk like him had sent her running.

"Was it like that for you?" he asked gruffly, knowing it was none of his business.

She looked at him, startled. "Was what like that?" she asked in a strangled voice.

Embarrassed, he realized she thought he was inquiring about their own ill-fated kiss.

"Were you and your husband romantic?"

She looked relieved. "Not really," she said with a small smile. "We were friends. We loved and respected each other. But fireworks? No, no fireworks."

She seemed to withdraw then, as if she felt as though she'd betrayed a precious memory.

He personally felt fireworks were pretty nice. And he'd sure as hell felt them the other day.

For some reason her response pleased him inordinately.

"Are you going to go talk to her?" Kate asked.

He shook his head. "Naw. I think he just sold a painting or something. Let them have their moment. I'll talk it over with the chief, but I'd like to just file another safe-and-happy report."

"I don't think her parents will be able to influence her anymore, even if they do find out where she is," Kate said. "The relationship is too strong now."

He thought about that for a moment. About the love between those two being so strong it was like a force that protected them from the world.

Maybe even a better force than loneliness.

"It was just like what you saw when I gave you her ring. The green truck, the water, the love, everything."

"I know. It's kind of scary, isn't it?"

He smiled. "Downright creepy."

She laughed.

He was so glad to hear her laughter again that he forgot all the tension between them. All he wanted was to be with her.

"How about if I buy you supper?"

"Oh, no," she said immediately. "Really, I—"

"Look, I've dumped my dog on you, gotten your help with my niece, taken you to Spokane and back and eaten you out of house and home. I think I owe you a dinner."

He could see that owing her something made it slightly more palatable to her than if it was like an official date.

And to him, too.

Who knew where an official date might lead? Maybe to a California-style home on Maple Tree Blvd. in small-town Sleepy Grove.

But this was different. Simple appreciation. Just saying thank you. After all, she was saddled with the dog again.

"All right," she said tentatively.

"Great, we'll just stop by my place, and I'll change into something else. Then McMurty's?"

"Oh, just a hamburger and fries would be fine."

But he didn't want to take her for a hamburger and fries, sitting in uncomfortable plastic chairs designed to make them move on as soon as they were finished eating.

He wanted to go to McMurty's and look at her in candlelight and have the waiter hand her a rose.

"Hamburgers and fries it is," he conceded, recognizing the danger of his own thoughts.

Kate wondered why on earth she was going for dinner with him. At least they weren't going to McMurty's where she'd have to look at those rough-hewn features softened unbearably by candlelight.

Candlelight might make her think of his lips and how they had felt, rough and demanding against her own. On the other hand, she should know by now that no candlelight was necessary to make her think those renegade thoughts.

They stopped in front of a nicely kept brick apartment with beautiful cedars lining the walks.

"Come in," he said.

"I'll just wait here."

"It's getting too hot to wait in here."

That wasn't true. It was a warm day, but not hot. Still, she did not want him to know she was a little afraid to be alone with him in his apartment.

She cast a glance at the sleeping dog.

"Don't worry about him," Hawk said. "With any luck he'll leap out the window and attach himself to some pass-erby."

He let them in the main door with a key. "I had the landlord install this," he said proudly. "They used to just leave this front door hanging open."

She wondered if the other tenants appreciated the security measure or were annoyed by it. Was Sleepy Grove ready for a man like this?

A man who had seen too much and done too much?

Was a small-town widow ready for a man like this? The kind of man who probably never would buy his own house and settle down?

He led the way up the stairs to his place. He opened the door with flourish, and she walked in gingerly, almost afraid of what his place would tell her of him.

She wasn't sure what she expected. Maybe buttery leather sofas, a big stereo system and lights that went down low.

But it was very apparent that Hawk was not that kind of bachelor.

His apartment pulled at some funny little place in her heart that she did not want pulled at, not by this big self-assured man, who was a whole lot more than she knew how to handle.

"Have a seat," he said, after they'd gone down the hall, passing a tiny galley-style kitchen that held an old arborite table, two battered chairs and one very well-used coffee-pot.

She paused at the door of the living room, trying to un-derstand why it made her heart feel so soft toward Hawk.

The living room had one wall partially painted a peculiar shade of mustard yellow. An even stranger shade of green was underneath that.

"I did the green mess," he admitted. "I decided I didn't like it partway through."

The couch was obviously new, overstuffed, gigantic sunflowers in the pattern.

"My sister wanted me to get something in leather, but I always feel like my skin sticks to it in the summer, you know? She called this one van Gogh's nightmare, but I kind of liked it."

A palm struggled for life near the window, and an indifferent mountain landscape hung on the long wall that was not mustard yellow and green.

"Wilma Nordstrom did the painting for me," he said with fondness.

Again some emotion she didn't want to feel tickled at her. All he could see in that painting was Wilma, the ugliness of the painting itself lost on him.

"Have a seat," he invited again, and she sank down on the van Gogh. It was wonderfully comfortable.

"I'll just be a jiff."

In a moment she heard the shower turn on and felt the heat rise in her cheeks. It was just too intimate to be sitting in his oddly enchanting disaster of a decorating effort, listening to the sounds of him showering.

If she tried, and she certainly wasn't going to, she would be able to imagine what that big body looked like unclothed, the water sluicing down through the matted hair on his chest, over the rippling muscles of his arms and legs and...

What had happened to her resolve to rid her life of him?

The resolve she had made when she had torn herself away from the compelling mystery and magic of his kiss?

Yet, here she was, sitting in his living room, listening to water she knew was drumming across his skin, looking at the painting he only saw caring in and listening now to his deep voice inexpertly singing a song about a man whose dog died.

Speaking of dogs, hadn't she been ridiculously pleased when Mrs. Johanssen had called and said the puppy wasn't working out? Her thoughts drifted to that boy and that girl at the side of the lake.

So in love.

Filling her with an aching yearning, making her so aware of an emptiness in her life, making her try to remember if she'd ever felt for Jerry what that girl so obviously felt for Mickey McGee. And then, unbelievably, Hawk had asked her that very question.

No. She had loved Jerry, but it had been a quiet kind of love. No fireworks, no love songs, no roses on Valentine's Day. He was a stable, wonderful man. He made her feel warm and secure and content.

Not red-hot and insecure and as restless as she had ever felt.

The bathroom door opened.

She held her breath, wondering if he would walk out dressed in only a towel.

Wondering and, some renegade part of her, wishing.

But he came out in tan canvas pants and a matching sports shirt.

"Ready for a hamburger at Joe's?" he asked.

Chapter Eight

"Everyone in the whole town must be here," Hawk said, surveying Joe's. "You know we could still—"

"I don't mind waiting," Kate assured him hastily, the idea of sitting across from him in candlelight more appealing than ever, therefore more necessary to fight than ever.

Joe's lacked any kind of romantic ambience. It was decorated in red and blue. The food was delicious, but the booths were backbreaking. People ate and left. It was not a place to linger. Thank goodness. Lingering around a man with eyes that particular stormy shade of gray might be habit-forming.

"Go ahead and find a table," he suggested. "I'll wait in line and place the order."

It was a form of new-world gallantry, considering the length of the line.

"All right. I'll have the Joe-Joe burger."

"And onion rings?" he asked smoothly.

An innocent enough question, really, unless one began to think of onion rings in the context of kissing, which of course would be a ridiculous thing to do.

"That sounds wonderful," she returned smoothly, as if kissing was the farthest thing from her mind.

He laughed, as if her thoughts were transparent to him.

"I think I'll have some, too," he said, something wicked in his eyes.

It would be ridiculous to read too much into that, too. She turned from him abruptly and went in search of a table. There was one close to the front. Faced with the choice of looking out of the window or looking at him, she chose him.

He was a glorious man to watch. He towered above most of the other people in the line, stood out and apart, radiating the confidence of a man who carried the burden of authority.

She noticed that every woman who came in the door focused almost instantly on him, some with veiled interest and some with blatant interest.

A woman in the line next to him smiled boldly. A woman much younger than he was.

That made things come back into perspective.

Kate was not the kind of woman a man like this went for. No, he could have the Cindy Crawford look-alikes and statuesque blondes.

She was not the type of woman who attracted that big, virile type of men.

She attracted men like Jerry, she supposed. An ordinary woman attracting the most ordinary of men.

She felt a pang of guilt at her own disloyalty, but it was still true. Jerry had been of medium build, slightly balding, glasses. He had not been the type of guy women gave second glances to. And it hadn't mattered one little bit.

Jerry's most wonderful features had been on the inside, not the outside.

Hawk surprised her by looking over his shoulder to see who the young lady was smiling at.

It endeared him to her in a way she did not welcome.

She saw a man and a woman come in with a baby and recognized the baby as Brittany.

She saw Hawk's sister was lovely, her hair dark and rich like his, her eyes as wide-set and beautifully gray. Her husband was one of those ordinary guys, like Jerry had been.

The kind of guys, she reminded herself, who had wives and babies.

The young couple spotted Hawk and went over to him, his sister handing him the baby right away.

Hawk took her with such obvious reluctance that Kate had to stifle a laugh.

A moment later he was at the table, the baby tucked under his arm in that football position he seemed to prefer.

He pulled Brittany out and popped her onto the table. "Remember Auntie Kate?" he asked.

Brittany gooed, and Hawk sat down on the seat right beside Kate. He was too big for the booth, and she could feel the heat radiating from him, the comfortable pressure of his leg on hers.

She silently asked for strength.

"They're joining us," he said in an undertone. "Is that okay?"

She detected it was not okay with him. Maybe she was not young and glamorous, but surely he wasn't ashamed to be seen with her? "Of course," she said.

A few moments later, after placing their order, his sister and brother-in-law joined them, and introductions were made. A high chair was located for Brittany, and she was strapped securely into place. She made wild grabs for Hawk's hair, which he deftly dodged.

"How is your father?" Kate asked Jack. She could feel Hawk stiffen next to her. "Hawk told me he'd had a heart attack."

Jack, shy and soft-spoken, filled her in on his father's condition.

"So," Mary said, when her husband had finished, "you've been seeing Hawk for a while, have you? Jack's dad had his heart attack—" She started counting on her fingers, and Hawk groaned low in his throat, a sound like an animal in pain. Kate slid him a look. Now she understood his reluctance to have his sister join them.

"Mary—" he said, trying to stop her, but it was the effort of a man who knew that he was already defeated.

"I just wondered!" Mary said, defending herself.

"We're not seeing each other," Hawk said hotly.

Kate was not sure she was glad he was clarifying the situation.

"We're friends," he finished.

And the way he said that soothed away the hurt of him saying he wasn't seeing her.

Which of course, he wasn't. Not with all those Cindy Crawford look-alikes giving him the eye.

"How did you meet?"

"Through work," Hawk said tersely, looking around as if the arrival of food might save him.

"Work?" Mary asked, surprised. "You're not in police work are you, Kate?"

"Mary—" Hawk said warningly.

"No, I'm not," Kate said, liking his sister despite her directness. Underneath it Kate was sure she saw a very genuine concern for Hawk and his well-being. "I'm a widow. I keep busy with my garden and some volunteer work."

"A widow," his sister repeated, and it was obvious to everybody she liked that better than a divorcée.

"Mar—" her husband said.

"How long have you been a widow?"

She was so transparent that Kate almost laughed, except it was too scary. Hawk's sister was obviously pairing them together in a very serious way.

"That's none of your business!" Hawk said.

"Six years," Kate said.

His sister gave a little mew of approval, and Hawk gave Kate a dark look before switching his attention to his sister.

"Mary, that's enough," Hawk said. "I've seen more subtle interrogations at the station."

His sister ignored him. "Do you happen to have a yellow couch?"

Kate blinked, startled. "Well, yes I do."

Mary smiled with satisfaction. "Oh."

"What does that have to do with anything?" Hawk hissed.

"I'm not sure," Mary said innocently. "It's just that you were so intent on a yellow sofa, and I wondered where you had seen one that—"

"Okay," Hawk cut her off.

"Do you happen to have green walls?" Mary asked.

"It so happens that I do," Kate said, enjoying Hawk's acute discomfort more than she knew she should be. It occurred to her that the fact one family had produced two people with such confidence was rather remarkable.

"A shade of olive khaki?" Mary asked with delighted disbelief.

Kate remembered the disaster on Hawk's wall.

"I'd have to say it's more moss-colored."

"Ah, moss," Mary said gravely.

The food came. Hawk dived into it as if he'd been on a thirty-day fruit juice fast. So did Mary's husband, Jack.

Mary looked over at her brother with affection and smiled. She winked at Kate.

"Have you heard about the Ladies Only dinner and auction next Friday?"

"Yes, I have," Kate said, noticing the twinkle of pure devilment in Mary's eyes.

"I understand they're auctioning bachelors," Mary continued sweetly. She looked directly at Kate, as though her big brother's reaction to this didn't interest her in the least.

"Yes, I understand that, too," Kate said. Out of the corner of her eye she watched Hawk start into his second burger, determined not to give his sister the reaction she was looking for.

"I think I'll go," Mary said.

Hawk slammed his hamburger down. "You're a happily married woman!" Then, remembering he wasn't going to react, he took a long draw on his milk shake.

Brittany made a grab for the shake, and Hawk, glancing blackly at his sister, obligingly gave her his used straw to chew on.

"It's all just in fun," Mary said easily. "How about you, Kate? Are you going?"

"I wouldn't miss it for the world," Kate replied.

Mary turned her attention to Hawk, and her nose actually scrunched up in disappointment when he didn't react in any way. In fact, he was quite engrossed in pouring milk shake directly onto Brittany's tray.

His delighted niece splashed in it and then licked her hands. Her eyes grew round with delight, and she tried desperately to cram her whole fist in her mouth.

"Was that tray clean?" Mary asked with dismay.

"Uh, gee, I don't know," Hawk said innocently. He smiled smugly when Mary leapt out of her chair, scooped up the baby and headed for the washroom.

"Match, game and set to me," he said of his sister's disappearance.

"That was just the opening skirmish," his brother-in-law informed him cheerfully. "Could you pass the ketchup?"

Hawk handed it to him, his brows lowered sternly. "You're not going to let her go to that stupid auction, are you?"

Jack laughed. "Let her? What century are you living in? If she wants to go, she'll go. It would be good for her to go have some fun."

Hawk glared blackly at his brother-in-law, then sighed. "I'm representing the police department at that auction, and I'd really rather she wasn't there. I'll never hear the end of it."

"You're right. You won't," Jack said placidly.

"I mean if the baby was sick or something—"

"Can't help you."

"I mowed your lawn while you were away!"

Jack grinned good-naturedly. "Thanks, Bill."

"Bill?" Kate interceded. The men obviously enjoyed each other very much. There was a rough affection in their sparring that was unmistakable.

It had been a long time since she had been part of a family. She had deliberately cut close ties by moving to such an out-of-the-way place.

She hadn't realized until now how she missed the teasing, the easy give-and-take of family gatherings.

"BIL for brother-in-law," Jack informed her.

Mary came back with a clean baby. She settled Brittany on her lap rather than putting her back in the high chair.

Hawk finished his last bite of burger. "Ready to go?" he asked Kate, obviously hoping to prevent the interrogation from restarting.

Her burger was only partially eaten, but somehow she didn't feel like it anymore. There was a funny ache inside her, a desire to be a part of something again.

A feeling she hadn't felt for a long, long time.

A feeling she was not certain she was at all comfortable with.

They said their goodbyes to an obviously disappointed Mary. On the way out the door, Hawk noticed the line had disappeared and bought two hamburgers for the dog in the car.

A small gesture. But it made her feel warm inside. What was this big, self-assured man doing to her heart?

Her phone rang later that night. Every time her phone rang she found herself hoping it was him. It was pathetic—just like being sixteen again.

"Is this Kate?"

"It is. Hello, Mary."

"Hawk cut our visit short. He's such a pain sometimes."

He was a pain sometimes. A royal pain in the heart. She refrained from sharing this sentiment with Mary.

"You know, Kate, I really felt like you and I could be friends. I'd like to get to know you better. Jack and I are relatively new here, too, and with the baby it can be hard to get out and meet people."

This was said very genuinely.

"I was wondering if you'd like to go to the fund-raising dinner together?"

Kate had a feeling Hawk would be most disapproving of the idea.

But it solved a problem for her. Like Mary, she knew very few people in town. She had dreaded the thought of going to that auction and sitting there by herself, like some poor desperate woman so lonely she had to buy a date. In fact, Hawk's asking her to attend the auction for him had made her realize how completely she had been isolating herself.

Oh, yes, she visited the old folks' homes. Those were nice safe relationships. They never went too deep. She was always the one in control. It made her feel like she had human contact, without having human involvement.

"I'd like that," she heard herself saying to Mary.

And it was only when she hung up she allowed herself to smile. At least part of the pleasure in saying yes was knowing how much it would irritate Hawk.

Kate had not dressed up for a long time. Oh, she wore her going-to-church-or-the-office kind of dresses, but the Ladies Only night was deemed semiformal to formal.

Going through her closets she realized that everything in them was outdated or carried too many memories. Here was the dress she'd worn to Jerry's sister's wedding. Here was one she'd worn to Jerry's last office party.

But it wasn't just the memories that made her reject each dress, it was what the dresses *said*. Settled. Happily married. Secure.

Boring.

And somehow, when she bought Hawk, she wanted him to look off that stage at all the sexy, attractive women who would be going wild for him and feel glad it was her who would buy him.

Even if it was fixed.

Even if it was his own money.

She ended up going to Spokane for the day. She had been planning to go, anyway, to talk to Sadie about a plan that had been slowly formulating in her head.

She shopped first. She found an incredible black dress in an upscale boutique. It was utterly sexy in its simplicity. It had narrow straps at the shoulders and a hemline just a touch high. The sales clerk assured her the dress had been made for her.

But she didn't need much convincing. When she looked at herself in the mirror, she saw a Kate who had never been. A Kate who had a wild side, a sexy side, a hungry side. The dress brought out the fire in her hair and the blush in her cheeks. It made her look glamorous and bold and very close to beautiful.

Quelling her doubts, she bought the dress and then began to worry the minute she left the store about what kind of message a dress like that would give.

She'd phoned Sadie in advance, and she met her at Giorgio's in time for Sadie's lunch break.

The younger woman looked thinner than ever, Kate noticed with dismay, and paler. The skin under her eyes was tinged blue with a weariness such a young woman should not have to experience.

They sat down together at a booth in the back.

"So, how's the cop?" Sadie asked awkwardly, searching for something to say.

"Oh, fine," Kate said, trying for nonchalance and feeling the heat go up her cheeks. Quickly she changed the subject, filling Sadie in about her brother and Samantha.

"Hey, I'm glad for them," Sadie said. She recommended the special, and they both ordered. Apparently she was not going to be distracted. "Is there something between you and that cop?"

"No!" Kate said, annoyed to see her very vehemence brought a smile to Sadie's lips. "We're just friends."

Sadie watched her. Not for the first time, Kate noticed the softness in eyes painted to look hard.

And she noticed the hard work and long hours adding up in the turn of the girl's mouth and the sag of her shoulders. Sadie didn't seem as spunky. She seemed sadder. Wiser. Wearier.

Kate took a deep breath. "Did you know I had a daughter who died?" It was the first time she had ever started a conversation like that. She'd always been busy running from the pain before. And yet saying those words didn't hurt the way she had thought it might.

"No," Sadie said softly.

Kate liked the girl's eyes so much. There was a sweetness there, a sensitivity she couldn't hide.

"Her name was Carly. She died in a car accident when she was just a baby. My husband died, too."

"I'm really sorry," Sadie said. The brightness of unshed tears lit her eyes. It made Kate absolutely sure she was doing the right thing.

"Sometimes when really bad things happen, you still want something good to come out of it," Kate said, amazed at how strong she felt, how very, very good. "The insurance company gave me a huge settlement when my family died. I've decided to put some of it into a scholarship fund."

"That's nice," Sadie said, looking away quickly.

Kate reached over and took the girl's hand. Sadie was not the type of girl who expected scholarships. Or kindness. Or anything.

"I'd like to send you back to school."

Sadie looked back at her. Her mouth fell open. For a minute there was something in her eyes so vulnerable Kate wanted to weep. But then it was gone. She drew her hand carefully out of Kate's.

"I wasn't very good at school."

"You finished. You graduated."

"I liked it," Sadie said wryly. "I just wasn't very good at it. I had to work really hard for a *B*. I mostly got *C*s. Kids with *A*s get scholarships."

"Not Carly's scholarship," Kate informed her firmly. "Marks are not always an accurate measure of the human spirit. I think you've got something special. I think you're wasting it here."

Sadie was silent for a long time, studying her hands as if she could not trust herself to speak. When she did, her voice had turned husky.

"The cop said that, too," Sadie said softly and with a certain amount of pride.

"I think he's pretty good at reading people."

Sadie gave herself a quick shake. "It's nice of you, but it's not in my nature to accept charity." This was said with stiff control.

Kate had anticipated this reaction. "If you paid it back when you were done school and had a good job, then we could give it to someone else."

Sadie's face was tight from holding back tears, and suddenly it collapsed. "All right," she whispered. After a long time she said, "You turned out to be my fairy godmother after all, didn't you?"

Kate smiled through the mist in her own eyes. "Maybe," she said.

Sadie reached out for her hand and squeezed it tight this time. "For Carly," she said with fierce determination. "I'll make it, you know. I always liked school, which is a big no-

no in my family. I never even hoped for college. Ever. It's not just that the money wouldn't be there, it's that they don't want anybody to pull themselves out of that muck."

"You've already started," Kate told her.

"You know," Sadie said, a certain stubborn set to her jaw, "I really hope everything works out between you and the cop."

"There's nothing between us," Kate said weakly.

Sadie nodded at the little bag from the boutique that was on the bench beside Kate. "You wouldn't be shopping there if there wasn't. You didn't pick no dummy to put through school, Kate Shea."

Two nights later Kate looked at herself in the mirror in utter horror. What had possessed her to buy this dress?

It was really a little wisp of nothing, something that a much younger woman should wear. It had been a stupid purchase. An attempt to be alluring that was utterly ridiculous.

Hawk had come over to feed Tex after his shift. He had not noticed what she was wearing then, and he would probably not notice what she was wearing now.

He *had* noticed that she still hadn't installed a dead bolt or peephole, and had gone immediately to the hardware store and picked up both items. It had taken him about twenty minutes to install them, cursing soundly the whole time.

She suspected he was venting his frustration about the auction.

"Shouldn't you go?" she had finally said. "You don't want to be late."

"There was a dress rehearsal for that stupid auction," he'd told her. "Frankly, Tim Ryan doesn't stand to gain much."

"Why?"

"There isn't exactly a huge pool of available talent," he'd told her grimly. "This isn't Miami. Not that I'm much of a judge of man flesh, but it seems to me most of those guys aren't worth a plugged nickel. Even Wilma seemed to be realizing she was in big trouble."

"Hawk, if that's the case, bidding could go quite high on—" she'd stopped, not knowing what to say. "On you," she'd finished weakly.

He'd looked momentarily pleased and then blacker than ever.

"How high do you want me to—"

"As high as you have to," he'd said grimly.

The doorbell rang just as she was slipping off the strap to change into the office party dress with the high neck and full skirt, in a lovely nonalluring shade of sky blue.

She hesitated, but the doorbell rang again. She pulled the strap back up and went to the door. Mary stood there, dazzling in red sequins. She held the door open and Mary stepped in. She looked at Kate, then looked around the room, then back at Kate.

"What a flair you have for creating atmosphere. No wonder he was making clumsy efforts to copy it. You look absolutely gorgeous, by the way."

Kate colored to the roots of her hair. "I was just going to go change. I feel like an idiot. I can't imagine what possessed me—"

"Forget it," Mary said firmly, taking her arm and leading her back to the coat closet. "You aren't changing. Which coat?"

"Well, that's just it. I don't even have a coat that matches and—"

Mary began shuffling through the contents of the closet as if she owned the place. Near the back she found a black shawl.

"Perfect," she declared, passing Kate the shawl she'd forgotten she owned. "Hawk is going to fall over dead when he sees you."

"Just the reaction I'd hoped for," Kate said dryly.

Mary laughed. "You can kiss him back to life."

Kate could feel that horrible blush coloring her features again. She hastily changed the subject.

"How did you know he was going to be there?" Somehow she couldn't imagine Hawk confiding his predicament to his sister.

"Jack told me. He can't keep a secret from me." Mary turned and gave a demonstration of her eyelid-fluttering technique, and Kate laughed. "So I figured out the rest. Hawk asked you to buy him. Great dress for the occasion."

"What makes you think Hawk asked me that?"

"Because you aren't the type that attends bachelor auctions," Mary said with an easy grin. "Not even for a worthy cause."

"And what type do you think I am?" Kate asked, not sure if she was amused or annoyed by Mary's assessment of her character.

"Oh, you know. The kind that putters around putting up pickles and growing begonias."

Amusement won out. Kate burst out laughing. "Oh dear."

"I think it's great," Mary said with utter sincerity. "Hawk needs a woman with a phony suntan and a sports car like I need a hole in the head."

"I don't think you should be deciding what your brother needs," Kate said uneasily.

Mary only snorted. "So he says. Ooh, what a fun night this is going to be. How much money did he give you? To buy him?"

"We just said we'd settle up later."

Mary smiled. "I think I'll push up the bidding."

"Don't you dare," Kate warned her and trailed her out the door, carefully locking her new dead bolt behind her.

The banquet room at the recreation center was packed. Kate felt terribly grateful that Mary had come with her. She would have hated being all by herself in this noisy room, full of dressed-to-kill women dead set on having fun.

Cocktails dragged on. Kate sipped a ginger ale. She was going to need her wits about her. Dinner was finally served and looked delicious, but Kate couldn't bring herself to do more than toy with it. The idea that Hawk was going to come out on the stage behind that royal blue curtain and that she was going to buy him was making her feel slightly ill.

She hated the spotlight.

Finally after dinner was cleared and a number of prizes had been given out and a few of the women had consumed a bit too much wine, Wilma Nordstrom took the stage, a battleship dressed in jade green velvet.

She welcomed them and told a few jokes and then announced the main event, an auction of North Idaho's most eligible bachelors.

But Kate knew the evening wasn't going to unfold exactly as anybody had planned when she saw what happened next.

The curtain on the stage lifted about two and a half feet, revealing a dozen pairs of bare masculine legs.

"Ladies," Wilma said to the stunned silence, "who will bid ten dollars on bachelor number one?"

A set of legs detached themselves from the line of legs, marching back and forth, doing a little jig.

Not Hawk for sure, Kate thought, as the room erupted into surprised laughter. It was evident that the identity of the bachelors would remain a mystery. Bidding would be done on the basis of legs.

Considering what Hawk had told her about the bachelors, the idea was nothing short of brilliant.

Considering her mission, it was nothing short of disastrous.

"Ten," a voice called from the back. The legs did a little skip.

"Twenty."

Kate scanned the legs that remained in a line in the background. Number two's were too skinny and white. Hawk would have tanned legs, wouldn't he? Coming from Florida? And muscular. That let out seven, eight and nine.

"What am I going to do?" Kate muttered out loud.

Mary managed to quit hooting for few seconds. "Third from the right," she said. "He got that big scar falling off his bike when he was twelve."

Nearly delirious with relief, Kate looked back at pair of legs number four. They were beautifully shaped legs, tanned and hairy. Sure enough there was a bad scar over the left knee. She felt weak with relief. Mary would know her own brother's legs. Though those number six legs looked very strong and healthy, too.

The bidding for bachelor number one, who had very skinny white legs, had already reached an astounding one hundred and twenty dollars.

At two hundred and sixty dollars the other legs shuffled off the stage and the curtain was pulled up, an inch at a time, to an audience gone mad.

Mr. Blain, the manager of Kate's bank, stood there in bright turquoise summer shorts and a T-shirt, pigeon-chested and beaming pinkly.

The audience applauded as though he were Brad Pitt. His buyer, a heavy woman in a neon orange dress, raced forward and claimed his hand.

The audience cheered wildly, and the fat lady kissed her prize.

Kate wanted to die. She was going to go up there in front of all these people whistling and catcalling and take Hawk by the hand and lead him away? A kiss was out of the question.

"I can't do this," she muttered.

Mary had her fingers between her teeth, which seemed to aid her in producing a whistle of amazing loudness. "Of course you can do it," she said happily. She shook her head. "I can see you and Hawk have at least one thing in common. You both take life too seriously."

Kate wanted to tell her that wasn't true, but the argument she came up with in their defense had to do with wrestling on her lawn, and she wasn't sure she should give Mary any ammo for her matchmaking guns.

But she did find herself wondering if they weren't the same in some essential ways. They both seemed content with simple pleasures. Bright sunlight on green grass. Watching the puppy play. Popcorn and a baseball game on TV. Hot tea on the front porch in the cool of spring evenings. Joe burgers and onion rings.

They were two people who did not belong in a place like this. Not even for a good cause.

Bachelors number two and three were dispensed with. Number two was the plump boy who stocked the grocery shelves, and number three was a middle-aged man who gelled his hair.

The atmosphere in the room was reaching fever pitch. Those number four legs showed a great deal of promise, long and well-muscled, sprinkled liberally with dark hair.

The legs stepped out of the line and stood forward. No skipping. No punctuating the applause and hooting with little dance steps. Just two legs planted rock solid in front of them.

Hawk, she thought.

The bidding was wild. It reached two hundred dollars in no time. Kate decided just to sit quietly, drawing as little attention to herself as she could. When the bidding had died down a bit, she would enter the fray. Unfortunately this did not seem to be the kind of auction where one could just tap their program against their cheek to make a bid. No, hands had to be waved wildly, and bids shouted out.

The bidding staggered to a near halt at four hundred and fifty dollars.

Taking a deep steadying breath and closing her eyes, Kate shoved her hand into the air. "Five," she called, her voice ringing out in an unexpected moment of quiet.

Silence. She opened her eyes. People were staring at her. There was a hum of whispered surprise.

Wilma Nordstrom, the town's most notorious matchmaker, slammed down the gavel and yelled sold before anyone else had a chance to counterbid. She winked widely at Kate, who now felt as if her face was on fire.

The remaining pairs of feet filed dutifully off the stage, leaving just Hawk's legs showing.

Slowly, playing the audience with wicked delight, Wilma raised the curtain.

The drape rose to show enormously long powerful legs, and then a pair of navy blue shorts, a naked torso that brought gasps and catcalls and whistles, a perfectly molded bronzed chest.

But somehow Kate knew. She wasn't even sure how, but she just knew.

The curtain was raised all the way to reveal the identity of bachelor number four.

His face, sculptured, beautiful, faintly embarrassed, was the face of a complete stranger.

Kate had not purchased Hawk Adams.

Chapter Nine

Mary was whistling wildly beside her. "Come on, Kate, go get him."

"Kate Shea," Wilma called through the microphone, "come and meet Michael O'Bryan."

How the heck did Wilma Nordstrom know her name? Kate was sure they had never met. She cast a wistful glance at the door. Beyond it, thirty seconds away, was cool air and silence—freedom. She wanted nothing more than to make a break for it.

But she squared her shoulders, knowing escape was impossible. Now she would just have to get through this ordeal with as much dignity as she could muster.

Reluctantly, feeling as if her feet were made of lead, Kate stood up. She grabbed her shawl off the back of her chair and wrapped it around herself, trying to hide as much of that I-need-a-man dress as she could. With her nose tilted upward, she made her way through the audience. She climbed the steps to the stage as though she were climbing the stairs to the gallows.

Michael O'Bryan, who looked all of twenty-two, was examining her with frank appreciation she found embarrassing. He was nearly naked, for heaven's sake. Mr. Blain had at least worn a T-shirt. Primly she crossed the stage to him and offered him her hand.

With a grin of pure devilment he ignored the hand. With astonishing swiftness he had one strong arm behind her shoulders and the other behind her knees. He tilted her over and scooped her up before she knew what had happened. The crowd was cheering with ribald enjoyment. To attempt to fight her way out of the brawny strength of his arms would probably only titillate them further.

Her shawl slipped from her shoulders and hit the ground, and her mortification was complete. She didn't think her life could get any worse, but it did.

Without warning, he kissed her square on the mouth, long and hard, trying to coax some response from her. The audience loved this. She was certain a riot would be more quiet. She thumped him soundly on his naked chest to get him to stop, and he was so surprised he nearly dropped her.

He set her down and her heel went over, making her stumble. Of course, the audience chose to believe she was swooning. Her strap picked that moment to fall down. She jerked it back into place, grabbed her shawl off the floor and turned to get off the stage as fast as she could. It was then that she caught sight of Hawk, standing in the wings, his arms folded over his chest, glaring at her with a look of such savage possessiveness it sent a ripple of heat right through the center of her being.

He too was wearing shorts, but he had covered his chest with a navy blue police department T-shirt. Maturity had made his chest much deeper than the chest she'd just been held against, and she was taken by a sudden impulse to run to him and bury her head against his solid frame.

But of course it was entirely his fault she was in this awful predicament to begin with.

She returned his glare, and to the accompaniment of wild stamping and applause left the stage. She might have at least accomplished her exit with some dignity if Michael had not been dogging her heels. He tried to take her hand as she walked back to the table, but she shook free of it impatiently.

Michael sat down in the empty chair beside her, obviously enjoying all the attention his naked chest was attracting.

"Hawk is really angry," Kate hissed at Mary.

"Good," she said back, unconcerned.

"You made that up about the scar."

"Yes, I did," Mary said unapologetically.

"Why?" Kate demanded.

"I don't know. I suppose I'm trying to force his hand, get him to admit what he feels about you."

"He doesn't feel anything about me!" Kate said, a touch shrilly.

"Yes, he does," Mary replied stubbornly.

"Mary, we just spent five hundred dollars of his money on the wrong man!"

"He's always trying to control everything. It'll do him the world of good to have things not turn out exactly according to plan."

Kate could see Mary was just one of those well-meaning, if somewhat aggravating, people who thought they knew what was best for everyone else. In her own way, she was probably every bit as controlling as Hawk, if not more so. "I can't imagine he'd want me to spend even more money."

Michael had been following the conversation with interest. He really was a good-looking boy, and he knew it.

"You bought me by mistake?" he asked with disbelief.

Kate sighed. She wished he'd go put on his shirt. "I had instructions to get Hawk Adams at any price."

"Oh, geez," Michael said. "I'm a fireman. I know Hawk. I suppose he's going to punch me in the face for kissing you."

"Of course he isn't," Kate said. "It's not as if we—" She stopped. What were they? Or what were they not? How did people phrase these things? He was not her boyfriend. He was not her live-in lover.

Mary was listening with avid interest to see what phrase she would use.

"We're just friends," she finished lamely. "I think I have to go. I can't spend any more money, and I can't face him. I just can't."

What she really meant was that she was tired of all the noise and all the attention. She was exhausted. She could not summon the energy to play this game again. If the town was going to chatter about her purchase of Michael O'Bryan, what would they say if she stayed and bought another man?

It was just too humiliating.

So she could not buy him, and she could not sit here and watch him be bought, either. Not even if it was all in fun. Not even if it was for charity. Not even if it was just for one date.

It occurred to her these were very strong reactions to a man she had just claimed she shared only friendship with.

It occurred to her that Mary had not just forced his hand, but hers as well.

In some far corner of her heart a tiny bell rang.

"Oh, no," she whispered.

"Come on, stay," Mary pleaded. "Aren't you just dying for Hawk's turn?" But she turned from her zealous inspection of the legs on the stage, looked at Kate's face and stopped. "What is it?"

The bidding was starting on number five. Kate was willing to bet Hawk was number six, and she planned to be long gone before the bidding reached fever pitch on that particular set of legs.

She leapt up. "Nothing," she said curtly.

But that wasn't true. Through the smoke haze and the women yelling and Wilma calling out bids, the bell was ringing, stronger now, clearer.

She loved him.

It was the most ridiculous place in the whole world to make such a shattering discovery, but nonetheless, the words were singing in her heart.

She gathered up her shawl with trembling hands and tried to slip from the room, but of course that was hard to do, since Michael was trailing her like a lost puppy, and everyone they passed had something to say about how quickly they were leaving.

Her cheeks hot, she realized she was going to be the town's laughingstock for weeks. The lonely widow couldn't wait to get out of there with that shirtless young buck.

But even that thought was small and paltry, nothing more than a background jangle like the noise of the enthusiastic women.

I love him.

Her cheeks felt like they were on fire, so she welcomed the coolness of the night when she was finally free of the building.

"You're blushing," Michael said, taking her car key from her trembling hand and inserting it in her car door.

"That was very embarrassing for me," she said by way of explanation.

He looked quite crestfallen. "At least you didn't get Mr. Blain."

"Oh, Michael, it wasn't embarrassing because I got you." Though that sloppy kiss in front of five hundred people hadn't helped. "I just hate the limelight."

She also hated what her heart was doing right now, fluttering like a butterfly caught too long in a net and suddenly freed, soaring upward on graceful wings.

"What do you want to do about our date?" Michael asked. There was a chill in the air that he was ignoring in a very manly fashion. "I mean if there's nothing between Hawk and you, you'd be crazy to let five hundred dollars go to waste."

He flashed big, straight teeth at her.

It was taking her energy to be with him. Energy she needed to explore that terrifying little secret in her heart.

"We are never going on a date," she told him quietly.

He looked dreadfully disappointed. What did a young man like him want to go on a date with an older woman like her for? She knew the dress had been a mistake. He probably thought she was far more worldly than she was.

His very own Mrs. Robinson. Ha-ha.

Still it was not his fault. He'd done a nice thing for charity.

"I'd like you to date somebody else," she said, with sudden inspiration. "Her name's Sadie McGee, and you'll have to go to Spokane. I want you to tell her exactly what happened, and then I want you to take her for the nicest dinner she's ever had, and then out to the theater or philharmonic after."

"McGee," he said slowly, and with just a touch of distaste.

"And I want you to treat her as if she's a perfect lady," Kate ordered sternly. "Pretend she's Princess Di. I'll call you with her number."

"All right," he said with a shrug. "If that's what you want. It's your five hundred bucks."

She managed to smile. "No. It's Timmy Ryan's five hundred dollars. You did a nice thing tonight, Michael. A good thing."

This seemed to mollify him slightly, and the last she saw of him he was running back toward the door, not having to be manly about his goose bumps anymore.

She drove home slowly, letting the silence seep into her, feeling the funny glow of that secret deep in her belly.

She realized she should pack a bag and leave town. Just until she regained her senses, just until she was thinking clearly. Instead, she parked her car and went up the walk and unlocked both locks on her door. She shed the shawl and went and looked at herself in the full-length mirror on the back of her bedroom door.

There was color in her cheeks and a glow in her eyes like she had never seen. The dress clung to her beautifully.

She knew she should take it off.

She knew she should take it off and change into her nicest pajamas, then crawl into bed and go to sleep. At least she should pretend she'd been trying to sleep when he came. And, knowing Hawk, he was bound to come straight over after the auction.

Or she could change into her pajamas and wrap herself in that big tentlike housecoat and put on the coffee and set out a big plate of those cookies he was so fond of. When he was done yelling about her purchase of the wrong man, they could sit around her scarred kitchen table and talk just like friends. Pals. Buddies.

She didn't change, and she didn't put on coffee, either. She eased her feet out of shoes that suddenly felt a size too small. She padded back to her living room, turned the stained-glass light on and curled up with her feet under her, and waited.

The room felt soft and golden. Carly's photo on the wall made her feel warmer inside than she already felt. It occurred to her that loving someone was not a betrayal of Carly, but an affirmation of her.

There was a knock on her door, but it was not a soft knock in keeping with her mood.

It sounded like if she didn't answer that door quickly, he was coming through it.

The soft haziness of her fantasies deserted her. What kind of fool was she, lazing around in a ridiculous dress waiting for Prince Charming's arrival? Of course she wasn't in love. She'd just been momentarily swept away by the bubbles in her ginger ale, by an evening too full of tension, an evening that had plunged her into a world so far from her own comfort zone.

She took great pleasure in delaying the moment she opened the door.

She looked out the newly installed peephole. Hawk stood there bathed in the pool of light from her porch, bristling with bad temper.

Her heart plunged to the bottom of her belly.

Unlike Michael, he had not charged out into the night in shorts. He was wearing jeans, faded nearly white, and a black leather jacket, the leather looking as soft as butter.

He looked tall and powerful and unbearably handsome.

But of course she could not let him see how vulnerable she was to him. The voice in her heart sang true, but what did it matter if his own heart was not singing an answering melody?

She flung open the door and crossed her arms over her chest.

"How could you not know who was me?" he bellowed without even saying hello.

"Mary gave me a bum steer."

"I should have known," he growled. "*You* still should have known. What were you doing with Mary? I could have warned you what a brat she was."

The dog came out of the kitchen, where he had taken to sleeping on the mat by the back door, and licked Hawk's hand.

"How long have you been letting him in the house?" he rumbled.

"A while," she answered back. "Who bought you?"

She said it casually, as if she didn't care.

"My troublemaking sister. Announced to the whole crowd I'd just become the world's most expensive baby-sitter. Is that kid here?"

"What kid?" she asked, baffled. "Brittany?"

"Of course not Brittany!"

"You're going to wake up my neighbors," she warned him.

"Is *he* here?" Hawk asked dangerously, lowering his voice only marginally.

"You mean Michael?" she asked with shock.

"Oh, now it's Michael. I suppose he's in the kitchen gobbling up chocolate chip cookies and drinking bat wing tea."

"As a matter of fact, he's not." He's jealous, he's jealous, he's jealous, a little voice sang joyously within her.

"He's not?" And then he masked his expression of relief by saying indifferently, "He's really very young for you."

"Thank you. I figured that out by myself. It's not as if I was so carried away by the masculine perfection of his legs that I bought him on purpose, forgetting all about you."

"You didn't?"

"I thought it was you."

"But how could you! I don't have legs like that!"

"I don't know what your legs look like, for heaven's sake!"

"You should have been able to guess."

"You're being unfair!"

"I know," he said, and a little smile twitched around the corners of his lips.

"It was awful for me, Hawk," she said softly, confiding in him. "When I saw it was him instead of you, I prayed for the earth to open up and swallow me."

"Me, too," Hawk admitted gruffly.

"He kissed me in front of all those people!"

"I saw," he said, and something flashed, cold and hard, through his eyes. It made her very glad she had never had to face him on the wrong side of the law, except of course for the illegal transport of lilacs, which hardly counted.

"Did you like it?" he asked, that same hard edge of danger in his voice.

"You watched," she said. "Did it look like I liked it?"

"That's not answering the question."

"That question doesn't deserve an answer."

"Why the hell not?" he asked, his eyes narrow and glittering.

"If I'm supposed to be able to recognize your legs, you're supposed to be able to recognize when I am utterly revolted."

"Revolted," he repeated with surprise. "Really? Revolted?"

"Not to mention humiliated. You couldn't tell?"

"Once that shawl hit the floor, I wasn't seeing much except red."

"Why?" she breathed, and the question shimmered in the air between them, and his eyes locked on her lips with such intensity she felt singed.

He chose not to answer. "I guess you're not going on a date with him, are you?"

"I asked him to take Sadie McGee and show her the time of her life."

"You did?"

She nodded.

Some carefully held tension left those big shoulders.

"That was a nice thing to do, Kate. I like that girl. I've been trying to think of a way to get her out of that bar."

The hardness was gone from him, just like that.

"I've set up a scholarship for her. She's going to go back to school in September."

He looked at her with such tenderness that she thought her heart would break for loving him.

"Can I come in?" he asked, like a man home from battle, looking desperately for a place to rest.

She wanted nothing more. Nothing. But she could not bring herself to say it. If he came in, how could she keep her secrets from him?

"Where do you think that's going to lead to?" she asked instead.

"Where it should have led to a long time ago," he answered quietly. "Can I come in, Katie Shea?"

"Yes," she whispered.

He closed the door slowly behind him and looked down at her gravely.

"You look pretty terrific in that black dress, Kate."

"You look pretty terrific in black leather, Hawk."

He reached out with one finger and gently snagged the strap. He pulled it down off her shoulder, leaned forward and placed a searing-hot kiss on her naked skin.

"When this strap fell down on stage, I thought I was going to march out there, throw you over my shoulder and carry you off."

"Why didn't you?" she whispered.

"I don't know," he retorted huskily.

"Mary told me you'd gotten that scar on your leg when you were twelve," she said stupidly.

"No scars on my legs. Want to see?"

She licked her lips and looked down.

His feet moved into her line of vision. She looked back up.

He was standing close, very close, looking at her with something that turned those cool gray eyes to hot pewter.

"Do you want to see?" he asked again, quietly, but there was no fun in his voice, a deadly seriousness that told her he knew how solemn a thing this was.

"Yes," she said hoarsely, and found herself being scooped up in strong arms for the second time that night, and to be honest about it, only for the second time in her whole life.

He was strong, his strength easy and unforced. It felt good to be in his arms, nothing like the way she had felt in Michael O'Bryan's, and there was more to it than just the absence of the crowd.

He found her bedroom without difficulty, and for a moment she wondered frantically if there was dirty laundry on the floor.

If there was, he didn't care. He laid her down in the middle of the white eyelet duvet that covered her antique four-poster bed.

His eyes never left her face, as his weight joined hers on the bed. He looked at her for a long time, his hand tangling gently in the curls of her hair.

She wanted to beg him to kiss her. And she wanted to bask forever in the way he was looking at her.

When he finally did drop his lips to hers, she was hungry for them, starving, and she met him eagerly.

Complete.

She had not known the emptiness that lived in her until now.

She had not known the size of the hole in her heart.

Complete. His lips on hers, the answering passion within her, his hands beginning the slow dancing caresses of her body, touching and stroking her arms and her neck as if his life depended on knowing her, all of her.

And then his need for a more intimate knowing became apparent, and somehow the straps of the black dress came down, and the dress came up over her head.

She looked at him, wide-eyed and silent, in nothing now but her camisole and panties. "Oh, Hawk," she finally whispered, "love me."

It was like a homecoming, two souls so lonely, and so afraid of caring, finding each other and circling closer and closer to this moment.

Of knowing.

Of knowing the world was not such a lonely place.

Of knowing that love was not such a scary thing.

Of knowing things would never be the same again, were being altered for all time with each breathless kiss and each stroke that brought them closer.

To knowing.

To completion.

He was beautiful. Muscular. Strong. Perfect.

But he was more. He was the man who had held Brittany and brought his silly puppy here and painted his walls yellow. He was the man who cared about Sadie McGee and Wilma Nordstrom.

Somehow, somewhere she had fallen in love with him.

And in this moment there was no place for caution with the tentative unfolding of that emotion.

He looked down at her. She was absolutely gorgeous in the soft, muted light. He felt like he'd been waiting his whole life to see this camisole that he'd been catching glimpses of for weeks now.

It was silk and lace, soft and beautiful as she was.

And unbelievably, he knew he couldn't do this thing.

The first time he'd caught a tantalizing glimpse of that camisole, or one very much like it, she'd been delivering lilacs, and he'd pulled her over.

He'd known the truth then. She was the kind of woman who went to church, who got married and had children and baked cookies and coached the little league.

She was not the kind of woman a man had a one-night stand with. Or a two-week fling.

Still, she was one hundred percent an adult, and she wasn't protesting. She wanted this. She wanted him as much as he wanted her. It was in her eyes, in the softness of her lips, in the rise and fall of her breasts.

With a sigh he took off his own shirt and gently pulled it over his head.

She was offering him a gift. Her love and her trust. He did not know if he was worthy of this offering or not.

"Can I just hold you tonight?" he asked gruffly.

He could feel some coil of tension relax inside her. So she was not as ready as she had pretended to be or thought she was. He lay down beside her on the pillows and pulled her close into the naked wall of his chest.

She snuggled there, in the curve of his arm, like a fluffy kitten. In what seemed to be seconds she was asleep, breathing deeply and evenly beside him, and he was staring at the ceiling wondering if he'd lost his mind.

"Usually," he muttered to himself, "when a man and a woman sleep together, they do more than sleep."

The door to the hall creaked open, and he heard the dog pad softly across the room.

It licked his hand that was hanging over the side of the bed, turned a few circles and lay down on the floor.

"Ah," he muttered, "domestic tranquillity." But his attempt at sarcasm was lost in the frightening chasm of his own yearning.

He awoke in the morning with bright sunlight splattered across the tangled sheets, catching in the red-gold of her hair. She was beautiful, more beautiful in the strong light of day than she had been in the muted shadows of last night.

He wanted to wake her with kisses, but there was no point in awakening the powerful urges within himself that he could not slake. He let her sleep, his eyes roving around the tidy coziness of her bedroom. Old things and lace.

What was he doing here? What was this tightness in his chest? This feeling of wanting to have this moment and make it stretch into forever?

What would it be like to wake up beside her forever?

He muttered a curse to himself, got up and pulled on his jeans, padded shirtless into her kitchen.

The dog followed him, and he let it out the back door.

If he'd thought to escape her, he was wrong. The room was now as familiar as she was. Comforting. A restful place to be.

Forever.

That dratted word again.

Well, there was no forever. He was a grown man, and he knew those promises were broken. In divorce courts. At grave sides. There was no such thing as forever.

But then just a little while ago, he'd have sworn there was no such thing as a woman who could hold a ring—or a Saint Christopher's medal—in her hand and tell him things about the person who wore it, either.

His thoughts drifted to last night. It was the closest he'd been in a long time to that boy on the dock. Last night his heart had been wide open, he had tingled with awareness of his own vitality, felt full to the brim with wonder. Last night he had acted with honor, that silly old-fashioned virtue he had possessed as a boy and had lost somewhere along the way.

He'd been wrong about her psychic abilities. Dead wrong. Maybe he was wrong about forever, too.

The direction of his thoughts made him very nervous, and he jerked open her fridge and looked in, as though he would find something there to distract his mind from the dangerous direction it was moving in.

He forced his focus onto those unstained glass shelves. She had milk and cream, juice, cheese, homemade jams, a little leftover chicken, lettuce, apples and grapes.

His fridge contained two cans of root beer.

It was a sign of incompatibility if he'd ever seen one.

Out of some form of belligerence he took the orange juice pitcher out and swigged straight from the jug.

There, he thought with satisfaction. That was what being free was all about.

But he felt no rush of exhilaration. In fact, he was left wondering what exactly was so great about it.

He snorted in self-disgust. The puppy whined to be let back in. He felt as though he was getting trapped by all this stuff.

That was it. He needed to get away for a few days.

What he had dreaded from the first moments of meeting her had happened. He was under her spell.

A few days at his grandfather's old cottage at the lake, with his dog and his fishing pole, and he'd be back to his old self.

Maybe he'd even go back to Florida.

He closed his eyes and thought of dusty palm trees and hot sun. Crowded streets. Gunfire. Tension. Loneliness.

Yessir, that was the life for him.

Swigging orange juice straight from the container and getting shot at.

He wondered how long it would take to arrange to go back. A couple of weeks, tops.

It was a bonus that he'd be out of Mary's meddling range.

Of course, he wouldn't see Brittany growing up, either.

In defiance of the squeeze of emotion that made him shiver, he took another swig of the orange juice, relieved that his future was decided. He heard a rustle behind him.

She was standing there in his navy blue police T-shirt, a tousle of hair falling over one eye, looking sleepy and happy and loved. The shirt ended mid-thigh and her legs looked absolutely gorgeous.

She seemed to find him drinking out of her orange juice jug very amusing.

His future wavered like the lines of a mirage.

"Good morning, Hawk," she said, her voice low and beautiful like a song of praise.

He could feel Florida slipping from his mind.

Run, an inner voice yelled at him.

"I'm going to go away for a few days," he heard himself saying remotely.

Oh, her eyes. Those beautiful green-gold eyes, the colors shifting and changing, and the sudden pain in them, the sudden haunted look so different than the look last night when she had gazed at him as if she could do so forever.

Forever.

"My grandfather left Mary and me a cottage," he said. "I thought I'd go there." And then from far away—it couldn't even be his voice, but dammit it was—he said, "Would you like to come with me?"

Chapter Ten

An hour later they were only approaching takeoff.

He deliberated this delay carefully. When a man wanted to go to the cottage he threw a six-pack of ice-cold cola, a bag of chips and two cans of stew into a brown paper bag. It took him more time to prepare his fishing kit than a gym bag containing one clean pair of underwear and a pair of socks.

But he'd invited her. It reminded him slightly of going somewhere with Brittany. An alarming number of supplies were growing beside her door. Fresh fruit, frozen juice, coffee, herb tea, several frozen steaks, potatoes for baking . . . she even remembered toothpaste and toilet paper.

Of course, he could have gone home and thrown a few things into a bag himself, but he didn't want to leave. She was still wearing his navy blue police T-shirt, and it looked so good on her that he wasn't going to ask for it back.

"Well," she finally said, "I'm going to take a shower and pack a few of my things, and then we'll be ready to go."

He hoped she'd invite him into the shower, but was glad when she didn't. To give in to this powerful urge to be close to her could lessen his ability to make sober choices. He was not sure that he could trust himself to do the honorable thing twice in a row.

"I'll run by my place and pick up a few things. I'll be back in twenty minutes."

"All right."

"I need my shirt."

She blushed to the roots of her hair, which he found very charming. Then she dashed into her bedroom, closed the door, then reopened it a crack and dropped the shirt out.

He'd known women who would have taken that shirt off right in front of him and waited to see what developed. He was astonished by how happy he was that she was not one of them.

He reached over and tugged on his shirt. The bedroom door remained closed. With a sigh, he went out the front door.

"Lock the door behind me," he yelled over his shoulder.

She didn't answer, and he didn't suppose she was going to run out and lock the door.

He turned toward the street and only then realized the enormity of what had happened last night.

One neighbor, a middle-aged man in a stupid hat, was out trimming a hedge that didn't need trimming. He stared at Hawk with open curiosity, but Hawk glared back until he looked away.

Coming down the street was one of the squad cars, moving very slowly. Miles Manhurst gave him a casual wave and a sly grin.

Across the street, curtains moved back an inch or two. He glared in that direction until they fell back into place.

He was here every morning looking after the dog. Why did they all seem to know he'd been here all night this time?

And of course they were all assuming *something* had happened.

"I hate small towns," he muttered to himself. He spent ten minutes at his place and was back. The neighbor with the hat pretended not to notice. The curtains across the street were now open, and a little old lady watered plants right in front of it. She pretended not to notice him, either.

If Miles made another sweep by, Hawk wasn't sure he could trust himself not to put a rock through the windshield.

She was ready when he stepped inside the door she hadn't locked. She was dressed in a pale peach shirt and light cream summer pants. Her hair was still wet and curling around her face.

She took his breath away.

And for some reason he didn't want her to know that.

"Your neighbors suspect the worst," he told her. "They were all snooping when I left this morning. And the police department had a spy out, too."

"I can't imagine why anyone would find us that interesting," she said casually.

He couldn't help but smile. He'd ruined her reputation in a single swoop, over *nothing,* and she wasn't the least perturbed. Or if she was, she wasn't showing it.

He loaded up the vehicle and then walked down the walk with her, tucking her hand into his.

He cast Kate a glance out of the corner of his eye.

Her chin was high. He squeezed her hand.

"Oh-oh," she said lightly. "It'll be all over town that we're getting married."

Still, she clung to his hand with a certain fragile strength that belied her easygoing words and tore unexpectedly at his heart.

Okay, he had already decided that this was not the type of woman you had an affair with.

But *married?*

He suddenly regretted asking her to join him at the cottage, regretted her boxes full of stuff, her neatly packed suitcases.

He needed time away from her, time away from the vulnerability in her eyes, time away, he realized, from his own vulnerability.

He needed to go back to Florida where he could be hard and cool and nothing touched the tough layers around his heart.

But glancing at her as he started the vehicle, he realized it might be too late for going back. He realized there might be only one thing as terrifying as the word *forever.*

Life without her.

He glanced at her again and felt a surge of warmth at the sweet familiarity of her face. He knew where every freckle was. He knew exactly how her lips moved when she smiled and how she flipped that one wayward lock of hair out of her eye when it fell forward.

He knew her and did not know her at the same time.

It could take a whole lifetime to know her completely.

By some odd coincidence, he happened to have a lifetime he didn't seem to be doing much with.

An invisible fist squeezed hard at his belly. What made him think that Kate Shea would have him?

Kate could feel the tension in him as they drove in silence. She realized she shouldn't have come.

She needed time to think. Oh, why had she been so impulsive? Why had she let him through her door last night?

Why hadn't she thought that by morning everyone who had driven by her place and seen his vehicle parked out front would be talking?

She should be too old to care if they talked.

But she wasn't entirely.

And now she'd agreed to go to this cabin with him, like two little kids playing house. No talk about the future, about *them,* just stumbling along hoping everything would work out.

How could it possibly work out, when she didn't even know what she wanted?

No, that wasn't quite true. She had loved waking up this morning with the scent of him in the air, the hollow in her bed where his big body had been.

She had loved coming into the kitchen, seeing the sunlight bronzing his naked chest, seeing him drinking out of the orange juice jug.

No, she knew darn well what she *wanted.* Day after day of him.

But further than that? Into the future? Did she really have the heart to start all over again with setting up a house with somebody else, balancing budgets with them, having babies?

Commitment.

She came face-to-face with her secret terror. Commitment.

She wanted to tell him to turn his vehicle around. Take her back. Let her go.

Instead she said nothing, sitting there as silently as him, terrified, as they drove toward an unknown future.

* * *

The cottage was beautiful, a lovely A-frame with windows facing the lake, a floor-to-ceiling stone fireplace dominating the design.

The cabin had been shut up since the previous summer, and it smelled stale. It seemed so suddenly to be just the two of them, at this cozy little lovers' retreat, with nothing to do but be aware of each other. And she was certainly aware of him and of the ache, the burning desire, the acute craving to be with him.

She bustled about opening windows.

There were two bedrooms, she noted, and he didn't seem to know what to do with the luggage. He set it in the middle of the living room floor.

Good grief, here they were in the nineties, two mature people who didn't have a clue how to progress with a relationship.

She turned to him when all the windows were open. The air smelled fresh and clean. He looked gorgeous, standing there in his faded jeans and his leather jacket.

Last night she had felt the satin of his skin next to hers, been kissed to sleep by him, dreamed in the curve of his arms.

She wanted for him to come across that room, gather her in his arms and kiss her senseless.

Because escape from her sensibilities would be a relief right now.

For a moment they stood frozen, staring at each other, the need naked between them.

"Let's go fishing," he growled, suddenly. "Have you ever been fly-fishing?"

She followed his cue willingly. They could put off defining a relationship for a while longer.

"No. I've dropped a pole over the side of a boat every now and then."

This disgusted him, and he rolled his eyes.

With the puppy gamboling along happily behind them, they left the cabin and went down to the dock.

She felt better almost immediately.

It was a beautiful day, the sun glinting off the deep blue waters of the lake, the cabins peeking out from under enormous trees all around them, the occasional boat out on the water.

She watched him take his fishing rod from a special case and put it lovingly together.

"This," he said of the rod, "is a work of art. Come stand here, on the left-hand side of me."

She stood and watched him as he let the line sing out over the lake, his arm moving it in gentle arcs over and over again.

Something happened to him as the line sang out. Some tension moved from him. When he turned his attention back to her she could see his face was relaxed. It was only then she realized how tense he'd been all morning.

"Come, I'll show you."

He had made it look easy, but in fact it was very difficult, and after a few flubbed attempts his arm went around her waist, his other hand covered hers, and together they made the line dance out across the water.

"You're getting it," he murmured. "That's it. Relax. Feel the motion. Feel the rhythm of it."

About all she could feel right now was the rhythm of his big heart beating beneath his shirt.

But the world felt right again. His closeness, the scent of him, the strength of his chest behind her, made everything all right. It chased away tomorrow and gave her just the moment in all its wonderful intensity.

His arms belonged around her. Rather than feeling awkward beneath his touch, it was like coming home to where she was meant to be.

Soon they were laughing and talking as she tangled the line and nearly put the hook in his eye.

By lunch they were starving, and they brought the basket of her sandwiches down on the dock and rolled up their long pants and dangled their feet in the water.

She caught her first fish after lunch, squealing like a child, partly delighted, partly horrified.

It was pathetically small, and he showed her how to let it go, cupping the small fish in his big hand and swishing it back and forth in the water until it was strong enough to give a sudden flick of its tail and swim away.

"I'm going to get my camera in case I catch another one," she told him, and raced up the stairs that led back to the cabin.

Inside she searched though her suitcase until she found the camera.

She turned to those huge front windows and framed a picture of the lake. In her viewfinder, she found him, his back to her as she focused on the dock.

Shocked recognition smashed into her.

The camera fell suddenly from her hands and hung from her neck. She staggered a few steps backward and sat in a big armchair, still able to see him.

He was standing on the dock, his back toward her. The puppy came from the trees, and she saw him turn and smile, his smile relaxed and full of life. The puppy came and lay quietly at Hawk's feet, his head on his paws.

It was him.

He was the boy who had fished on this dock long ago.

It had been his Saint Christopher's medal she had held in her hand.

The feeling welled up in her. Of loving him.

Of having always loved him.

Of having always known that this was meant to be.

What was she going to do?

She closed her eyes, and for a single frozen moment she could see Carly smiling at her, beaming.

She opened her eyes, feeling shaken, but knowing what to do.

He turned when she finally came down the dock toward him, and held up a big fish.

"Supper."

"Great."

"Is something wrong?"

"Not at all."

"You're looking at me oddly."

"Am I? I think I'm trying to see the boy you once were." He was silent.

"A boy who wore a Saint Christopher's medal."

He ducked his head slightly.

"And stood on this very dock, with his dog and his fishing pole."

"Oh, yeah, that." He put his rod down and sat on the dock, patting it beside him. "Yeah, it was my medal. I didn't know you then. I was kind of testing."

"And?"

"Everything you saw was true. The happiness of that boy. His freedom. Even the fact he'd become lost in the man."

She sat down beside him. Her heart was beating too fast inside her chest.

"It's funny it came up, because I feel like I have a choice to make now," he continued softly. "Whether to return to those lost parts of myself or give them up forever. Bury them."

"Don't do that, Hawk."

"I've been thinking of going back to Florida."

It felt as if he had taken his fists and slammed them into her stomach. She battled the tears that threatened to fall. She stared out at the lake, refusing to look at those handsome features, the face that could make her beg.

"You know that boy? Mickey McGee?"

She nodded stiffly, not trusting herself to speak.

"I didn't like him, and I finally figured out why. He's like what I once was, free, unfettered by convention, alive. And he's not going to lose it, either."

She felt as if she was choking. Like some part of her was holding on to her tears so hard that the effort of it would choke the very life out of her.

His next words were completely unexpected.

"Kate, I'm scared to death."

She did look away from the water then. Looked into his grave features and knew he spoke the truth. He was afraid. This man, who had faced bullets and danger of all kinds, was sitting beside her on a dock, and he was afraid.

"Of what?" she managed to ask.

He turned and looked at her. The pain in his eyes was so real. "Us."

She nodded tightly, looking away.

"Kate, I'm in love with you."

She actually felt her heart stop beating.

"I love you in a way I haven't loved anybody since I was that boy standing on that dock."

She turned to him swiftly, her mouth falling open. She snapped it shut.

"I don't know anything about loving people," he said painfully. "I don't know anything about being gentle or considerate or caring. I'm a cop."

She trembled beside him. It would have been easier if he just said goodbye. So much easier.

"You could become a widow twice before you're forty."

They both knew something had just crept into the conversation, uninvited. The future.

"I love you," he stumbled on. "But I don't deserve you. And I'm really messy."

This last statement was so absurd and said so pathetically, and yet of all of the things he had said, it was this one that gave her hope.

He didn't want to go. He wanted to stay.

It occurred to her, with a flash of insight, that he didn't think she would have him.

"I drink straight out of the milk container," he warned her darkly, "and I leave my clothes on the floor. I don't have any eye for color at all. None."

He was scowling at her ferociously. She noticed that feeling of being about to burst into tears had evaporated. She slipped her hand into his and felt him squeeze it as though she'd thrown him a life preserver.

"I love you, too, Hawk. With my whole heart and soul."

He stared at her. "Are you kidding?"

"No."

"You should have more sense."

"Somehow I think these things aren't always sensible."

"Now that you love me back, it's really scary."

"I'll bet," she said with a certain dryness.

"I could die on my job, you know."

"Yes, I know."

"Well then, I was a damn poor choice to fall in love with."

"I've loved you ever since I saw the boy on the dock. My heart knew even then it was you."

"It did?"

"You know, Hawk, I had a safe life once, as safe as I could make it. My husband wasn't in a job where he had any chance at all of dying. But he did die. And I learned there's only so many things people control. Some things, maybe even most things, are beyond us. Beyond our control, beyond our ability to understand."

"No kidding," he agreed vehemently.

"This is going to sound crazy to you—"

"As if anything could be crazier than falling in love with the town's soothsayer—"

"But it feels like it was all so I could meet you."

"All what?"

"Seeing things, being able to feel things. I feel like it was a universal design leading me to this moment, sitting here beside you, loving you."

He was looking at her with such gladness she could feel the tears in her eyes again.

Suddenly she heard a sound and swiveled her head toward it.

"What?" he asked.

"Did you hear that?"

"No. What?"

She shook her head. "I thought I heard a baby laugh."

"If my sister is here with Brittany I'll—"

"Shh, listen, Hawk."

She could hear it again, faintly, far away, like angels tinkling small bells in blessing.

"Did you hear it?" she asked.

"No," he said gruffly. "I don't hear anything." He reached up with one strong, long finger and caught the tear rolling down her cheek.

"It takes more courage to love people than to live in isolation," she whispered.

"I know. I've stood on the wrong end of a gun before, and it never felt like this."

"And yet it feels like this...this one moment sitting here next to you, loving you, will give me the courage to do whatever else I need to do with my life."

"You need to marry me," he growled.

There it was. The answer to this relationship dilemma. And it was so wonderfully simple. She smiled shakily at him. "I do," she agreed, "I need to marry you."

"That takes courage," he joked.

"It does," she joked back.

"I come with a puppy that isn't house-trained. And a niece who isn't, either."

She laughed shakily as his arms wrapped around her, pulling her close to him.

"Of course, I could be using you to guarantee I never have to be in another bachelor auction."

"Yes, you could be," she murmured.

"And so I can move out of that apartment that I've darn near ruined."

"No doubt about it."

His lips grazed hers. "Did you put a spell on me, Kate?"

Her laughter tinkled over quiet waters. "Kiss of the Lilac Lady."

"I've always been really afraid of this funny little word. *Forever.*"

"It's just a word," she assured him huskily.

"No," he said, "it's not. It's a feeling. And the only thing scarier than forever would be forever without you in it."

He was right. It was a feeling. This feeling that was inside her right now. A feeling that had nothing to do with words.

A feeling of being in the right place at the right time. A feeling of being looked after by a benign universe. A feeling of all being right with the world.

A feeling that life and death and love, especially love, all have meaning, all being part of a tremendous and colorful tapestry, vibrating with warmth and energy.

"I don't feel scared anymore," he said. "Just happy. The way I used to feel when I came here as a boy. Funny, that it should come full circle like this."

"I think love moves in circles. Circles of life. Circles of death. Circles of healing."

"Wait here a minute." He was gone just a short while, and when he came back he sat beside her and slowly opened his hand.

In it was a beautiful band of gold, glowing softly.

"It was my mother's wedding band," he said softly. "When she died, I put it in the cabinet in the cabin. She loved it here." He hesitated. "I'd like you to have it.

"I mean, if you want it. If you'd rather have something with diamonds and—"

She shushed him and took the ring from the palm of his hand. It was beautiful gold, pliable in its purity.

She gasped with soft surprise at the magnificent warmth coming from the ring.

"Do you feel something?" he asked.

She closed her eyes. She expected she would see his mother, but instead she saw him, in soft focus, his back to her, standing on the end of this very dock. The sound of a baby laughing was louder than ever.

A boy of four or five, sturdy and dark-haired, was running along the path to the dock, a mature German shepherd guarding his every step.

"Daddy," he cried, as his feet hit the dock.

Hawk turned, and it was then she saw the fat baby strapped to the front of him in one of those baby pouches.

Hawk's face, as he turned to the boy who had called him Daddy, was softened with the most incredible light of love.

"Do you see anything?" Hawk asked again.

The vision faded. Kate blinked and opened her eyes. She slid the ring onto her finger. It fit perfectly.

She looked at him, deeply, lovingly. The future was right there, in his eyes.

"Yes," she whispered. "I see paradise."

*   *   *   *   *

Silhouette ROMANCE™

COMING NEXT MONTH

Conveniently Wed: Six wonderful stories about couples who say "I do"—and *then* fall in love!

#1162 DADDY DOWN THE AISLE—Donna Clayton
Fabulous Fathers
Jonas's young nephew was certainly a challenge for this new father figure. But an even bigger challenge was the lovely woman helping with the little tyke—the woman who had become this daddy's wife in name only.

#1163 FOR BETTER, FOR BABY—Sandra Steffen
Bundles of Joy
A night of passion with an irresistible bachelor left Kimberly expecting nothing—except a baby! The dad-to-be proposed a *convenient* marriage, but a marriage of love was better for baby—and Mom!

#1164 MAKE-BELIEVE BRIDE—Alaina Hawthorne
Amber was sure the man she loved didn't even know she existed—until the handsome executive made a startling proposal, to be his make-believe bride!

#1165 TEMPORARY HUSBAND—Val Whisenand
Wade's pretty ex-wife had amnesia—and forgot they were divorced! It was up to *him* to refresh her memory—but did he really want to?

#1166 UNDERCOVER HONEYMOON—Laura Anthony
Pretending to be Mrs. "Nick" Nickerson was just part of Michelle's undercover assignment at the Triple Fork ranch. But could she keep her "wifely" feelings for her handsome "husband" undercover, too?

#1167 THE MARRIAGE CONTRACT—Cathy Forsythe
Darci would marry—temporarily—if it meant keeping her family business. But living with her sexy cowboy of a groom made Darci wish their marriage contract was forever binding....

Take 4 bestselling love stories FREE

Plus get a FREE surprise gift!

Special Limited-time Offer

Mail to Silhouette Reader Service™

- 3010 Walden Avenue
  P.O. Box 1867
  Buffalo, N.Y. 14240-1867

YES! Please send me 4 free Silhouette Romance™ novels and my free surprise gift. Then send me 6 brand-new novels every month, which I will receive months before they appear in bookstores. Bill me at the low price of $2.67 each plus 25¢ delivery and applicable sales tax, if any.* That's the complete price and a savings of over 10% off the cover prices—quite a bargain! I understand that accepting the books and gift places me under no obligation ever to buy any books. I can always return a shipment and cancel at any time. Even if I never buy another book from Silhouette, the 4 free books and the surprise gift are mine to keep forever.

215 BPA A3UT

Name	(PLEASE PRINT)
Address	Apt. No.
City	State	Zip

This offer is limited to one order per household and not valid to present Silhouette Romance™ subscribers. *Terms and prices are subject to change without notice. Sales tax applicable in N.Y.

USROM-696   ©1990 Harlequin Enterprises Limited

SILHOUETTE... Where Passion Lives

Add these Silhouette favorites to your collection today!
Now you can receive a discount by ordering two or more titles!

SD#05819	WILD MIDNIGHT by Ann Major	$2.99	☐
SD#05878	THE UNFORGIVING BRIDE	$2.99 u.s.	☐
	by Joan Johnston	$3.50 can.	☐
IM#07568	MIRANDA'S VIKING by Maggie Shayne	$3.50	☐
SSE#09896	SWEETBRIAR SUMMIT	$3.50 u.s.	☐
	by Christine Rimmer	$3.99 can.	☐
SSE#09944	A ROSE AND A WEDDING VOW	$3.75 u.s.	☐
	by Andrea Edwards	$4.25 can.	☐
SR#19002	A FATHER'S PROMISE	$2.75	☐
	by Helen R. Myers		

(limited quantities available on certain titles)

	TOTAL AMOUNT	$_____
DEDUCT:	10% DISCOUNT FOR 2+ BOOKS	$_____
	POSTAGE & HANDLING	$_____
	($1.00 for one book, 50¢ for each additional)	
	APPLICABLE TAXES**	$_____
	TOTAL PAYABLE	$_____
	(check or money order—please do not send cash)	

To order, send the completed form with your name, address, zip or postal code, along with a check or money order for the total above, payable to Silhouette Books, to: **In the U.S.:** 3010 Walden Avenue, P.O. Box 9077, Buffalo, NY 14269-9077; **In Canada:** P.O. Box 636, Fort Erie, Ontario, L2A 5X3.

Name:_____

Address:_____City:_____

State/Prov.:_____Zip/Postal Code:_____

**New York residents remit applicable sales taxes.
Canadian residents remit applicable GST and provincial taxes.

Silhouette®
TM

SBACK-JA2

Silhouette's recipe for a sizzling summer:

* Take the best-looking cowboy in South Dakota
* Mix in a brilliant bachelor
* Add a sexy, mysterious sheikh
* Combine their stories into one collection and you've got one sensational super-hot read!

Summer Sizzlers

MEN OF *Summer*

Three short stories by these favorite authors:

Kathleen Eagle
Joan Hohl
Barbara Faith

Available this July wherever Silhouette books are sold.

Look us up on-line at: http://www.romance.net

Silhouette®

™

SS96

You're About to
Become a

Privileged
Woman

Reap the rewards of fabulous free gifts and benefits with proofs-of-purchase from Silhouette and Harlequin books

Pages & Privileges™

It's our way of thanking you for buying our books at your favorite retail stores.

PROOF OF
PURCHASE
Offer expires October 31, 1996

SR-PP148

Pages
& Privileges ™

Harlequin and Silhouette—
the most privileged readers in the world!

For more information about Harlequin and Silhouette's PAGES & PRIVILEGES program call the Pages & Privileges Benefits Desk: 1-503-794-2499

Silhouette®

SR-PP148